CALYX
BOOKS

KILLING COLOR

KILLING COLOR

Charlotte Watson Sherman

CALYX BOOKS ▼ CORVALLIS, OREGON

The publication of this book was supported with grants from the National Endowment for the Arts, the King County Arts Commission, and the Oregon Arts Commission.

Cover art "I am Free," acrylic and watercolor by Jody Kim
Cover design by Carolyn Sawtelle
Book design by Cheryl McLean

CALYX Books are distributed to the trade through major library distributors, jobbers, and most small-press distributors including: Airlift, Bookpeople, Bookslinger, the Distributors, Inland Book. Co., Pacific Pipeline, and Small Press Distribution. For personal orders or other information write: CALYX Books, PO BOX B, Corvallis, OR 97339, 503-753-9384.

∞

The paper in this book meets the guidelines for permanence and durability of the Committee on Production Guidelines for Book Longevity of the Council on Library Resources and the minimum requirements of the American National Standard for the Permanence of Paper for Printed Library Materials Z38.48.1984.

Library of Congress Cataloging-in-Publication Data

Sherman, Charlotte Watson, 1958-
    Killing color / Charlotte Watson Sherman.
        p.   cm.
    ISBN 0-934971-18-8 : $16.95. — ISBN 0-934971-17-X
(pbk.) : $8.95
    1. Fantastic ficton, American. 2. Afro-Americans—fiction.
3. Supernatural—Fiction. I. Title.
    PS3569.h415K5 1992
    813' .54 — dc20   91-34341
                                                                CIP

Printed in the U.S.A.

Acknowledgements

The author wishes to acknowledge Craig Lesley, Margarita Donnelly, Cheryl McLean, the CALYX staff, the King County Arts Commission, the Seattle Arts Commission, and Artist Trust for making the dream of this book a reality.

Special thanks to Colleen McElroy, gracious mentor and *une femme ancienne sauvage.*

Thanks to Barbara Henderson, Faith Davis, Jody Kim, JoAnn Moton, Tina Hoggatt, Lenore Norgaard, Perry Ulander, and Brenda Peterson for continuous inspiration and support. Thanks to Addei and John Bernard for sharing their computer wisdom.

I am most grateful to my family: Charles Watson, Dorothy and Harold Glass, Lois and Alton Sherman, Erika Sherman, Richard and Michael Glass, David, Aisha, and Zahida Sherman.

And to *Les Prisionieres D'Amour* — Carletta, Nancy, Julia, Colleen, Martine, Raina, Marilyn, and Marsha.

For David, Aisha, and Zahida
and in memory of Zackel and Bessie Harrison

PREVIOUS PUBLICATIONS

Earlier versions of some stories were published in: "Swimming Lesson," *Obsidian II,* Volume 4, Number 1, Spring 1989, and "Killing Color," Volume 4, Number 2, Summer 1989; "Cateye," *Seattle Arts IMAGE,* November 1988; "Killing Color," *Memories and Visions: Women's Fantasy and Science Fiction,* Crossing Press, 1989; "Pink Dolphin," *Upstream: The Literary Center Quarterly,* Spring 1991; "Emerald City: Third & Pike," *Permafrost,* Volume 9, Number 2, Spring 1987; "Talking Mountain," *Portland Review,* Volume 35, Number 2, April 1989; "A Season," *Painted Bride Quarterly,* Number 37, 1989; and "Killing Color," *CALYX, A Journal of Art and Literature by Women,* Volume 12, Number 3, and "Swimming Lesson," Volume 13, Number 3.

Contents

INTRODUCTION

In the tradition of Buchi Emecheta, Simone Schwarz-Bart, Toni Cade Bambara, Isabel Allende, and a host of other women writers who are storytellers, Charlotte Watson Sherman spins tales that are part magic, part song. In eleven stories of magnificent presence, Watson Sherman casts reflections of a world too often turned upside down by its own special vision, a world in which passions quicken and fold, resting palpably upon the page. These stories are fashioned in a language that links image and music, and though it may appear somewhat confusing to speak of such a clear narrative voice as Watson Sherman's as a voice of song, the most haunting, most meteorical facets of *Killing Color* are its music and translucent energy. These stories do not contain songs of sorrow or pop rhythms that backdrop inertia; the songs in these stories are equipped with a centrifugal rage below the surface, a siren's cry of love and sensuality, a child's wonder and the vulnerability of innocence.

Ah aa um ah oo u.m is kind of how it sounded, Chango, like if you close your eyes and listen to the sound of the universe breathing, that was the sound of my mother's tears.

"A Season"

...pieces of words they membered from when we was all free sound like: hmmhmm o-o o-o-o-o mlongo. And the wind would start to blow and the trees on the edge of the riverbank would start to sway....

"Swimming Lesson"

Josephine started to hum, an old sound each of the others in turn pushed into the circle until it melted into one long hum rolling over the water. "BigWater"

Way on into their lovin Nathan whispered, "O way o way, o way o wayo," into the sweat coverin Leah's neck like dew.

"Cateye"

The songs are wellsprings, songs of primordial authenticity that run, like veins, through the stories. And each story, in its own fashion, stands as an invocation to the spirituality of African American women, women who see themselves as gloriously female, as Viola does in "Spirit Talk" when she describes herself as *Lookin finer every day. So, I'm a little soft round the edges? I'm soft and tough as leather, soft on one side, tough on the other. Like a real woman.*

These are women who *do not breathe alone,* as Albertina Woods cautions in "The Pink Dolphin"; they question their roles, refusing, as Oya does in "Emerald City: Third & Pike," to accept judgments against them, or, as Albertina epitomizes, to accept age as a lessening of their femaleness: *...tall at eighty-eighty, strong-voiced with wrinkleless skin the color of palmetto berries, her laughter, a strong dark wine.* We see what ennobles these characters, what instills in them a sense of optimism. *You are never truly alone, you know.... Here, breathe deep,* Watson Sherman reminds us as she presents us with women who are infused with a sensuality that nearly dances off the page.

Right away I started gigglin and actin silly even though I left my girlhood behind fifty years ago. It just seem like I never had a chance to be a girl like this and then Tad would start up to ticklin me and nobody passin on the road woulda guessed that the muffled snortin lovin sounds was comin from two folks with all kinds of wrinkles over they bodies.

"Killing Color"

These women are in touch with themselves as well as with the geography that nourishes them. The ritual of coming of age, in "BigWater," is irrevocably tied to place. When the women *stepped from the darkness of the trees onto rocks shining like skin holding water*, their christening becomes a christening of the earth as well. *This is the place we come to be women*, Keta's mother tells her. *This is the place we come to be whole.*

Indeed, the landscape is so important that the story, "Talking Mountain," fuses place and character: *...that mouth opened and made the sound of a mountain choking*. And *Tavio looked into the eyes of this man and saw something breaking inside them, earth crumbling and falling in upon itself....*

No fictional form can present more difficulties than the short-short story, but such is not the case with "Talking Mountain." The instrumentation of the narrative voice reverberates in this four-page story. It begins with a simple proclamation: *Magdalena has no tongue*, but its consequences are far reaching. The story is finely wrought and chilling, so tersely written it is as if we have seen figures projected through an old-fashioned camera obscura, where movements persist on remaining a step out of synch as the world tries to catch up with itself.

Magdalena had looked into the dull eyes of countless numbers of children, eyes that were small worlds that passed like her days, eternal barren planets on parade.

"Talking Mountain"

Magdalena has nowhere to run, and neither do we. We are hooked to the intimacy of relationships that marks the social resonances of this collection. The uniqueness of Watson Sherman's characters rests on their tendencies to stand at the edge of communities, outside of the norm, the expected. In these stories, we see characters who are rooted in a space between history and the future, like the tree in "Floating" that *Reverend Daniles swears covers a hole leading from this world to the next.* But often those roots take a turn that cracks the surface of the landscape, and it is then that we see the larger social reality where class/caste is the bully pulled by racism through the streets of the community.

In some instances, the caste mark is the fabric of the story's spirituality. Both "Cateye" and "Spirit Talk" offer an ancient metaphorical vision of a child fathered by spirits. The symbol for "Cateye" is the caul, the archetypal midwife's element. In "Spirit Talk," Watson Sherman focuses on physical features, particularly hair and eyes, the proverbial distinctions of post-colonial racial hierarchy. And in both stories, the symbols endow their owners with a double vision that is both a blessing and curse.

Despite Viola's attempts with *her own portions of white blood to erase from Reba's mind any memory of Basil's talk about the glorious African past,* Reba shaves her head and dons a wig because *she never felt her father had meant for his African queens to have blond hair.* "Spirit Talk"

One day Eldridge asked Miss Ophelia why everybody cept his mama and daddy called him Cateye. Miss Ophelia pulled him to her softenin bosom and said, "Cause you got them pretty yella eyes, baby. You got soft eyes that glow when people look in em and folks always like to put a name on things they don't understand so's they don't be scairt. "Cateye"

Watson Sherman chooses as her strongest symbol the eye, its vision and what it looks after—how it perceives the world. Like the ancient goddess Maat, whose name is based on the verb "to see," Watson Sherman's eyes see beyond the visible horizon where the world is sometimes cold as death, sometimes fiery as the sun.

Sometimes Oya's eyes look red and wild, but she won't say anything to anybody. Other times her eyes are flat, black and still as midnight outside the mission, and she talks up a furious wind. "Emerald City: Third & Pike"

Mavis turned them yella eyes on me. Now, I heard stories bout people talkin with they eyes and never even openin they mouths, but I never met nobody like that before.

"Killing Color"

And the daughter of the long lost Nola Barrett says: *One time at supper I made the mistake of trying to tell her how pretty I thought her eyes was, but she raised herself up like a rattler in her chair and hissed, "Shut your mouth, you old wrinkled-up raisin, fore I put you in a box and sell you to Miss Lomax to eat."* ... *Everybody at the table laugh when she say that. They scairt not to.* "Floating"

Watson Sherman offers us a vision of a special world which is vital, dynamic, even puzzling. But as Albertina tells us, we must *breathe deep* and inhale the heady fragrances of *Killing Color*, all the while feeling privileged to be caught in these stories, in the wild dance of laughter, the rooted sorrow and intimacy as she spins a web, a tale, a song that keeps us turning, turning long after the music has ended.

Let your hips sway to the sound, feel it flowing in your veins ah oo um ah oo um ah oo um. Pick up your feet and put them back down heavy ... like you are digging yourself back into the earth, back into your mother, back home where the silence is paradise and there are no fields no guns no children growing into machines. "A Season"

Colleen J. McElroy

The spirit cannot descend without song.
African Proverb

Swimming Lesson

I like to sit on this big old mossy pillow and lay my head back on one of them twisted red oak roots that look like arms comin up outta the ground, arms that feel like the satin of Aunt Leatha's skin when she stoops down to gather me up and swing me round, and I lay in the roots like I'm layin in my mama's lap, listenin to her hum them old old songs, sound like folks bottled up with sorrow so sweet it turn to sugar.

This tree's right next to the old black pond where sometimes we get out in the water that covers our skinny arms with sparklin oil and we splash and kick and laugh.

I member the day somebody got the crazy idea to throw Neethie in the water and try to make her swim, and we all knew it was the wrong thing to do and didn't think bout what grown folks always say bout if you know better do better. We didn't think bout that when we was way out in all that green by the black water neath that big old red sun, but we shoulda, like I told everybody what would listen later. But nobody listened, not Egghead Sammy Ray Yarbrough, not even C.C. Beauregard whose daddy runs the funeral parlor and everybody is scairt of him cause he might get mad and get his daddy to come for ya in the middle of the night and put ya in that old

1

hearse look like a big fat shiny beetle and take ya to the funeral parlor and put ya in a casket. So nobody, not me, not Elmo, not Ruby, not nobody said a word when Egghead Sammy Ray Yarbrough and C.C. Beauregard decided they was gonna make Neethie swim.

Now, anybody got half a piece of sense know Neethie can't swim, don't like the water, can't even walk right on land on accounta one leg bein shorter than the other and don't nobody usually say nothin bout it one way or nuther cause that just the way she come into the world, lookin kinda like a crookedy upsidedown wishbone. But some folks be laughin bout that big-sole shoe she gotta wear on her short leg so she don't walk lopsided. But she still limp a little even with that big shoe on. I like Neethie even though she do live in the Bible most of the time.

Mama always say ain't nothin wrong with Neethie livin in the Bible and wrinkle up her face and tell me I need to live in it too and ask me don't I want to enter the Golden Gates of Righteousness? I say I only wanna enter the golden arches of that shiny new hamburger stand they got there in Jackson and she won't even let me do that.

But we probably wouldn'ta thought to put Neethie in the water if Ruby hadn'ta been talkin bout how Jesus could walk on water. C.C. Beauregard said: No he can't, can't nobody walk on water. But I told em what my playuncle Eaton told me bout the slaves in the old days who left beatins and hoein and cotton and cleanin and set out cross the fields and headed north where they thought they could be free, and how some of em come to that yellow river that flow not too far from here and thought they had come to the end of they journey cause they couldn't swim and didn't know what all was in that water. Then they'd stoop at the edge and wet they faces

2

and start moanin pieces of words they member from when we was all free, sound like: *hmmhmm o-o o-o-o-o mlongo*. And the wind would start to blow and the trees on the edge of the riverbank would start to sway and the air would feel like how my mama say it feel sometime when Reverend Samuel hit a high note in the middle of his preachin, and the women start to tremble and the deacons start to shake and everybody's eyes start to water with tears rollin down. That's how my playuncle Eaton say it feel when the run-aways bent down at the edge of the yellow river thinkin bout freedom and how they couldn't swim and hummin: *mlongo mlongo hmmhmmhmmhmm o-o*. They knew they couldn't turn back so they kept on hummin that song and then they feet sank in the red mud at the edge of the river and come up covered with green sprouts climbin on they ankles and circlin round and tiny wings grew from each ankle and started flappin back and forth and back and forth, gentle at first and then faster and faster. And they could feel the cold of them chains deep in the wet earth and the wings beatin harder and then they took a step into the yellow water but they first foot didn't go down. It stayed right on top of the waves, and they put they other foot in the water and the same thing happened, it didn't go down, and they look over they shoulder for they last look at the land that tried to turn em into mules. They know they wouldn't never turn back, so they kept on walkin and the tiny wings kept beatin and they glided on cross the yellow river and only got the bottom of they pants and dresses wet.

But then Sammy Ray Yarbrough, whose head's big as a jug of water, broke in with his silly self and said, "Can't no slaves or nobody else walk cross no water, not even with wings on they back," and he don't believe Jesus did it neither. Ruby said she's gone tell his mama he said that, so he said o.k., if Neethie can walk on water, then anybody can cause Neethie was the closest thing to Jesus any of us knew bout. C.C. Beauregard said he'd go and get Neethie and bring her to the pond.

Now me and Ruby and Elmo tried to shift round and act like we wasn't scairt, but I knew we all musta been thinkin bout the whuppin we was gonna get when our mamas found out we'd pushed Neethie in the water, specially since she had a short leg and had to wear that big old shoe. I wasn't sure but it sound to me like this was cruelty and mama always say cruelty's one of the worst things in the world. Anyway, after a little while here come C.C. Beauregard holding Neethie by the hand and pullin her through bushes the color of bloodstone.

Soon as they got up to where we was standin near the edge of the pond Elmo started cryin, but didn't nobody pay him no mind cause Elmo always start cryin whenever somethin's bout to happen, good or bad. Mama say that boy just like to cry.

But when C.C. Beauregard brought Neethie to the edge of the pond I could feel tears wellin up in my own eyes, cause I knew it was gonna be one of them whuppins what hurts for a long, long time, probably one with a switch, cause Neethie was dressed up in a white ruffly dress that looked like it was for Sunday school, had her hair curled all over her head and had on some black patent leather buckle up shoes that was shinin like a mirror. I could see the trees and the sun when I looked down in them shoes.

Now Neethie's eyes was full of all of that kindness from livin in the Bible. And folks never made much over her short leg in front of her. She looked like some kind of

4

brown angel standin there by the pond holdin C.C. Beauregard's hand.

"See, I told you I'd tell you what I brought you to the pond for, didn't I?" C.C. Beauregard asked.

"Uh huh," said Neethie.

Nobody else said a mumblin word. It was pretty quiet cept for the crickets whistlin and a few birds talkin in the trees and frogs croakin. We wasn't gonna say nothin and I was hopin Neethie have sense enough to turn round and go on back home, but C.C. Beauregard told her he was gonna teach her how to swim so she could come out and play with us at the pond every day steada goin and sittin up with the Bible and all them old folks all the time. Then he asked her wouldn't she like that?

"Uh huh," Neethie said.

So then C.C. Beauregard told her the onliest way for him to teach her how to swim was for him to see if her body was heavy in the water and the only way he could tell that was if she stepped out on that log and walked clear back to us. Egghead Sammy Ray Yarbrough'd found a short log and pushed it up to the edge of the pond where it lay in the water lookin like a big fat link sausage.

Neethie said, "You want me to walk out on that log and walk back on the water like Jesus?"

And C.C. Beauregard said, "Yeah, I want you to walk back just like Jesus."

Well, what he go and say that for? I didn't know whether to laugh or cry so I just started hummin that sound my playuncle Eaton told me was magic: *mlongo mlongo hmmhmmhmm o-o.*

Neethie started to get out on the log and Elmo started to holler. Ruby started cryin real soft-like where you almost

5

couldn't hear her, what with Elmo's screamin and the wind whistlin in the trees.

C.C. Beauregard said, "Neethie, you think you better take that big shoe off?"

Neethie didn't say nothin, just looked kinda sweet and pitiful with her big black eyes lookin out on the water.

Now we all knew she couldn't swim a lick so if she fell in, there was gonna be hell to pay as my daddy say when I'm in double trouble. My legs started to itch and I could already feel that switch, but I just kept on singin: *hmmhmmhmm o-o mlongo.* When Neethie was at the end of the log, she dropped her head back and looked up into the sky and said, "I believe." That was it. Just "I believe," and me and Ruby and Elmo with his cryin self all held hands and stood in a kinda circle at the end of the log, and C.C. Beauregard and Egghead Sammy Ray Yarbrough started movin back to the trees slow and easy. And then Neethie turned round and looked at C.C. Beauregard and asked, "You ready?" And that crazy boy just looked at Neethie with his eyes poppin out and didn't say nothin. So me and Ruby started singin them old magic words and Elmo was so scairt he stopped cryin and started singin em too: *mlongo mlongo hmmhmmhmm o-o.* The words that was old magic went deep inside Neethie, deep inside, and Neethie stepped off the log into the air and put her foot down on that black water and she stayed up even with that big shoe on. Me and Ruby and Elmo squeezed our hands tighter and pressed our eyes shut, and sang the words louder and louder: *mlongo mlongo hmmhmmhmm o-o.* And the words pulled Neethie on cross the water and when we opened our eyes, Neethie was standin right there with us, her smile big as Egghead Sammy Ray Yarbrough's head, cept he wasn't there to see it.

Well, I thought that woulda fixed C.C. Beauregard and Egghead Sammy Ray Yarbrough good, but they didn't even get to see Neethie walk on water cause they slipped through the trees and run off soon as she stepped off the log.

We told Neethie it was good they was gone, cause they probably wouldn'ta knowed what they was lookin at anyway.

Then Ruby said, "Let's go over to the Sunflower Ice Cream Shop and get us some sodas to celebrate."

"Celebrate what?" Neethie asked.

"Us all not gettin the whuppin of our lives," I said, and naturally Elmo started cryin.

CATEYE

 his was sacred ground. And somethin in the land called out to Nathan Honeywood soon as he stepped his broken-soled, heavy brown shoes down from that train.

Somethin liquid and light as air snaked its way from his soles, round his ankles, and up into the muscles of his calves. It wiggled up his thighs and tickled his groin, makin him wanna laugh, but he wouldn't cause he didn't want folks to take no notice of a big black man laughin and holdin his privates. So he let the chuckle stay and started walkin.

And the light liquid thing walked right with him: past the bustle of the town, the friendly shouts of merchants, past the fabrics displayed in windows reflectin Nathan's smile, past the smell of hot bread bakin and fresh vegetables spread on tables, and still Nathan walked.

The liquid light rose from his navel and drifted into his chest. Nathan walked by vacant lots and leanin shacks. He hadn't seen this much green since he left Mississippi. And trees! Everywhere he looked there was a tree reachin for the silver sky. And he could smell salt water in the air.

Nathan and the light thing walked till he saw other brown faces with eyes that looked like they knew where he'd been and just how long the road had been to get here.

The thing in him rose into his throat like a thick ball of fog and his eyes watered and he started whisperin, "O way o way, o way o wayo," even though he didn't know what he was sayin. The thing in the land knew Nathan was home.

Nathan found his way to Miss Mary's roomin house. Miss Mary was a little pinched-up honey-colored woman who liked to hum to herself steada talk to people.

If a roomer asked her a question, she hummed the answer to herself and the listener had to listen real careful to catch on to what she was sayin. This didn't seem to bother most folks since the rooms was clean and the cost didn't put a hole in a body's billfold.

From Miss Mary's hummin he found out bout the wagon what took men out to the loggin camp once a week every sunup and brought em back when Friday night turned to Saturday.

Miss Mary hummed to herself, "You look like a man what done worked from can't to can't."

Nathan just grunted and went back to his room.

After workin in the camp for a year and keepin to hisself all the while, Nathan noticed a woman the color of simmerin chocolate had moved into Miss Mary's. And from listenin to Miss Mary's hummin at the supper table on Sunday, he found out her name was Leah. Nathan took to rollin her name round on his tongue like somethin sweet and too good to swallow. The camp had turned his big body lean as the lumber he fed into the cuttin machine. His stomach was flat and tight, his arms and legs solid. The softness of the woman, Leah, could fill the big open spaces surroundin Nathan Honeywood.

Miss Leah Barnett was what folks call a travelin woman. She'd picked up her feet from the farm her folks'd had since slavery days and started walkin. She stopped and worked a while in whatever town her feet stopped pulsin in. Then when the wind whispered, "Soooo far, sooo far, sooo far to go," she started walkin again.

This city sparklin with green and silver light was as far west as she had the spirit to go. She was relieved when the wind finally whispered what sounded to Leah like, "Go slow, go slow." Leah went so slow she decided to stop for good.

Nathan took to walkin with Leah on Saturday evenings. He liked the way she looked movin her full body through the open space easy as a tall pointed ship partin the sea. He enjoyed the sound of her words fallin from her lips, the way her mind whirred like a fancy machine. The day he asked her where the round tuft of white hair in the middle of all the crinkly black hair had come from and she told him it was somethin painted on her so she could read the wind, he knew she was a kindred spirit.

They stood before the makeshift minister and said the words. Then they went back to Nathan's room and moved into each other like the sea breeze circlin the city. Nathan was night openin over Leah and Leah was earth takin rain into its pores.

Way on into their lovin Nathan whispered, "O way o way, o way o wayo," into the sweat coverin Leah's neck like dew.

There was a string of baby girls that come, but none of em was breathin by the time they fell from Leah's body. Nathan tried to act like it didn't matter much, but each dead baby left a crease in his face. Leah now wore the stunned look of a bride and kept on pushin pecan-colored baby girls out of her stomach.

When Nathan finally stomped his foot and said, "We both had enough, Leah," Leah conceived for the last time. She kept tellin everybody this child was different, the way she was holdin this baby was new, that this child felt different deep inside her belly.

Nathan just looked at her with fog in his eyes and a face carved with sorrow. But Leah was right, this child was different, cause it did breathe when it left Leah's body. This one was a maple-colored boy with yella eyes that looked like they was glowin.

Nathan and Leah put together enough money to buy a small house. Leah stopped takin in wash after the baby came and breathed outside her body. They called the boy Eldridge, after Nathan's great-grandfather, Eldridge Honeywood, but everybody took to callin him Cateye.

Nathan and Leah and Eldridge was pretty happy livin on their little spot of land and growin prosperous as the town grew into a little city. The days passed like they pass in any other place, some slow and chewy like taffy and others quicksilvery. When Eldridge was ten years old, Leah's mama come to live out the rest of her days with the Honeywoods.

Ophelia Barnett was a woman with years of hard work carved into her spine. Her hands was hard and wide as any man's, and Eldridge was wary of her at first.

But by and by, he came to cherish Miss Ophelia's frisky sense of humor. She loved laughin and jokin, mockin the way folks talked and how they looked and walked. She often had Eldridge rollin on the ground, gaspin for breath with her stories bout the animals on their farm.

Sometimes Nathan and Leah would sit out on the porch on warm Indian summer evenins, when the days passed like the tails of red velvet evenin' gowns, and marvel at the child they had made.

Though Nathan had tried to make Eldridge hard like he thought a man oughta be, Eldridge was soft in the core and Leah was pleased. She believed men oughta have some woman in em and women oughta have some man in em.

The thing in the land that first grabbed holt of Nathan when he stepped off that train was still in him, and he thought it had gotten into Leah from the way they loved, but he wondered if the liquid light was gonna get into Eldridge and keep him on this land, or if he was gonna turn out like his mama and be a travelin man.

One day Eldridge asked Miss Ophelia why everybody cept his mama and daddy called him Cateye.

Miss Ophelia pulled him to her softenin bosom and said, "Cause you got them pretty yella eyes, baby. You got soft eyes that glow when people look in em and folks always like to put a name on things they don't understand so's they don't be scairt."

Eldridge turned this thought over in his head till her answer satisfied him.

Then one day he was puttin a pot of water on the stove to heat for his mama and he looked inside the pot and saw webs draped all cross his forehead.

Eldridge screamed and jumped back and looked inside the pot again. There they was, hundreds of silvery webs crisscrossin the top of his head.

He screamed again and ran to the water closet and scrubbed at his face till his skin was hot and raw. Miss Ophelia rushed into the closet.

"Whatsa matter, baby?"

Eldridge looked at her with panic in his eyes.

"The webs, Miss Ophelia. The webs! They all over my face and I can't get em off."

Eldridge kept rubbin at his skin. Three large pearls of blood glistened in the middle of his forehead. Miss Ophelia looked at the webless face in front of her and the strainin yella eyes. She pulled Eldridge to her.

"That ain't no spider web, baby. It's a veil and you the only one what see it. And you know what? It means you a very special boy who's gonna turn into a very special man."

No one talked bout what Eldridge had seen on his forehead. And Nathan didn't wanna hear nothin bout no veil on his child. "This world's hard enough to live in and try to figure out without havin to worry bout another one too."

And so the days passed. Eldridge turned twelve and was walkin home from school one day with Wonzell Gleason when his mind handed him a vision. Wonzell's brother fell out of a tree and rolled cross Eldridge's mind like a movin picture.

"Your brother's gonna break his leg," he said.

Wonzell looked at him as if he was crazy and didn't say a word. They kept on walkin. Wonzell wasn't at school the next day and it wasn't till the next week that Eldridge found out Wonzell's brother was sittin in an apple tree when a crow flew at his head and he fell to the ground and broke his leg in two places. Eldridge tried to erase the memory of the movin picture that had streaked across his mind.

Months went by without any more movin pictures and then one evenin when Eldridge sat on the porch with Thomas Grant, a boy he caught snakes with, a picture of Thomas' mother with only one eye drifted cross

Eldridge's vision. He turned to Thomas.

"What happened to your mama's eye?"

Thomas looked at Eldridge as if he was losin his mind.

"Ain't nothin wrong with my mama's eye. What's wrong with your mama's eye?"

Eldridge felt foolish for sayin anything and tried to calm Thomas down fore they got into a fight.

After Thomas went home, Eldridge felt uneasy. He went into Miss Ophelia's room. She was not as big as she was when she first come to live with em, but you could still see the strength in her narrow arms. Miss Ophelia was the only one he could talk to bout this crazy thing inside his head.

"Miss Ophelia, I saw Thomas Grant's mama with only one eye. What you think that mean?"

Miss Ophelia motioned for Eldridge to come sit by her bed. She held his hand.

"Well baby, I don't rightly know. Maybe we should wait and see if it mean anythin at all."

When Leah came home from the dry goods store and told them Bessie Grant had been kicked in the face by a mule and lost her right eye, Eldridge went into his room and got into bed. Miss Ophelia came into the room quietly.

"It's a gift you got, baby. A very special gift. You can see things with them yella eyes the rest of us can't see. It ain't nothin to be scairt of, just somethin that makes you you. We all got somethin make us special and your seein's what you got to give the world."

Eldridge looked at Miss Ophelia for a minute, then yelled into the darkness, "I don't want no gift. I don't wanna see things other folks can't. I don't wanna be special. I just wanna be myself."

Miss Ophelia's voice had tears in it when she said, "But you yourself, baby. You yourself with a funny kind of twist. You just gonna hafta come to a place in your heart where you can accept it."

And she left the room.

Months passed, years passed, and Eldridge didn't see any more movin pictures inside his head. Then two weeks before his fifteenth birthday, Eldridge stopped talkin to everybody and took to stayin in his room.

Nathan, Leah, and Miss Ophelia could hear him in there snifflin. Nathan and Leah was worried, but Miss Ophelia tried to calm em.

"He can see things, that's all. Things we can't see. Right now it hurts him, but one day he'll come to understand."

The night fore he was to turn fifteen, Eldridge crept into Miss Ophelia's room.

"I keep seein mama in a long skinny box. She's asleep and I can't wake her up."

Miss Ophelia grabbed Eldridge and held him as she cried. Eldridge didn't have no more tears. They both knew what was comin.

They say after his mama died Eldridge didn't go round folks no more, didn't go to town, wouldn't talk to his friends. Nothin.

He still live on that street shaped like a horseshoe, way back in the bushes, in a old square box of a house with only one window. If you walk past the path leadin up to the house when the wind blows, you can hear all them chimes he got hangin on his porch, soundin like a long holy song in the breeze.

Some say it was his daddy what made that boy see things like he do. Others swear on everythin good they hold in their souls that the seein come from his mama. I don't know where it come from, but I do know you could look in that boy's eyes and see whole worlds inside em.

Guess the only ones he'd talk to was his daddy and Miss Ophelia, and after they was gone he just stayed up in his house.

Don't none of us hardly ever see his back, let alone them yella eyes.

KILLING COLOR

For Beulah Mae Donald, a Black woman who won a $7 million judgment against the Ku Klux Klan for the murder of her son Michael, who in March 1981, at the age of 19 was strangled, fatally beaten, then had his body hung from a tree. Mrs. Donald was awarded the United Klans of America, Inc., headquarters property in Tuscaloosa, Alabama. She died September 17, 1988.

They say they got trees over seven hundred years old down in that yella swamp where even the water is murky gold. Bet them trees hold all kind of stories, but ain't none of em like the one I'm gonna tell bout Mavis.

Now, I'm not sayin Mavis is her real name. That's just what I took to callin her after seein them eyes and that fancy dress. Mavis had so much yella in her eyes it was like lookin in the sun when you looked right in em, but a funny deep kind of sun, more like a ocean of yella fire. You was lookin on some other world when you looked in Mavis' eyes, some other world sides this one.

I first saw Mavis leanin up against that old alabaster statue of some man my Aunt Myrtice call George Washington, but I don't think so cause it's got this plaque at the bottom bout the Spanish-American War and George Washington didn't have nothin to do with no Spanish-American War.

Anyway, I don't like talkin bout that statue too much cause it just gets Aunt Myrtice to fussin and I was always told it ain't right to talk back to old folks, so I don't. I just let her think she right bout things even though I know better. Still, that statue's where I first seen Mavis, and seem like don't nobody know where she come from. We just look up one day and there she was, leanin against that alabaster statue of not-George Washington.

I ain't no fancy woman or what some might call a hell-raiser, but I know a woman full of fire when I see one, and if somebody hadda struck a match to Mavis, she'da gone up in a puff of smoke.

Mavis got honey-colored skin look like ain't never had nothin rough brush up against her. She had on some kinda blood-red high heel shoes. She the kind wear genuine silk stockins with fancy garters to hold em up, nothin like them old cotton ones I keep up on my leg with a little piece of string tied round my thigh.

Now she was wearin all this right here in Brownville, in the middle of town, in the noonday sun when all you could smell was the heat risin. So naturally I stopped and got me a good look at this woman leanin up against that statue with her eyes lookin straight out at that old magnolia tree front of the courthouse.

Most of us folks in Brownville try our best to look the other way when we walk by that big old barn of a court-house. In fact, old Thaddeous Fulton, who I likes to call myself keepin company with, won't even walk on the same side of the street as the courthouse, cause most of us know if you brush against the law down here, you sho'nuff gonna get bad luck.

But Mavis was lookin at that old courthouse buildin full on with them yella eyes of hers never even blinkin, and she did it with her back straight like her spine was made outta some long steel pole.

When Tad come round that evenin, I tried tellin him bout Mavis standin up lookin at the courthouse, but he just shook his head and said, "Sounds like trouble to me." He wouldn't talk bout it no more, which got me kinda mad cause I like to share most of my troubles and all of my joys with this man, and I don't like seein his face closin up on me like he's comin outta some bad story in a book. But that's just what he did when I tried tellin him bout Mavis.

That man had somethin else on his mind for that evenin. I could tell by the way his eyebrows was archin clear up in his forehead.

Tad's slew-footed as they come and was born with only half his head covered with hair, so the front of his head's always shinin like a Milk Dud. But can't nobody in all of Brownville match that man for kissin.

Seem like he tries gobblin up most of my soul when he puts them sweet lips of his on mine and sneaks his tongue in my mouth. I nearly fell straight on the porch floor the first time he give me one of them kisses, and it wasn't long fore we got started on one of our favorite pastimes—debatin bout fornication. We always waited till Aunt Myrtice dozed off in her settin chair fore we slipped out to the porch and started up our discussion.

"Now, Lady (he likes to call me Lady even though it ain't my given name). Lady, I done lived a good part of my life as a travelin man, and you know I lived in Chicago a good while fore I come back home. And things everywhere else ain't like they is in Brownville. People be different. I knowed quite a few women that was good women. Good, decent women. But we wasn't married or nothin.

We was just two good people tryin to keep they bodies warm in this cold, cold world. Now what's wrong with that?"

"Well, the Good Book say that them livin in the lusts of the flesh is by nature the children of wrath."

"I done seen more of life and people than ever could be put in a book. And I ain't never met nobody that died from lustin with they flesh. What I did see was folks full of wrath cause they wasn't gettin no sin."

"Well the Good Book say..."

"Lady, I don't b'lieve in no such thing as the Good Book cause I know there's lots of ways of lookin at things and you can't put em all in one book and say this be the Good Book."

"Watch out now, Thaddeous Fulton. You can't come round my house blasphemin."

"I still don't b'lieve in no such book. But I do b'lieve in a good life full of love. Now come on over here and give me a kiss."

Right away I started gigglin and actin silly even though I left my girlhood behind fifty years ago. It seems like I never had a chance to be a girl like this and then Tad start up to ticklin me and nobody passin on the road woulda guessed that the muffled snortin lovin sounds was comin from two folks with all kinds of wrinkles all over they bodies.

Tad always ask, "Well, if it's really the Good Book, then shouldn't everything that feel good be in it as a good thing to be doin?"

"That depends on what the good thing is cause everything that feels good ain't good for you," I always say.

"But Lady, look at all the bad that's out there in the world. Folks gotta have some things that make em feel good. Things gotta balance some kinda way, don't they?"

And I always agree there needs to be some kinda balance to what's good and what's bad. Then Tad always starts talkin bout how good he feels just lookin at me and listenin to me talk bout the world.

"I try to show you how much I preciate you with my lips," he say and give me one of them devilish kisses. "Don't that feel good?" he ask and then keep on till we whisperin and kissin and doin pretty near what the Bible calls fornicatin out on the porch.

▼▲▼▲▼

The next day I went to town and there Mavis was standin in the same spot by that statue, lookin at the courthouse.

Folks was walkin by lookin at her and tryin not to let her see em lookin, but Mavis wasn't payin nobody no mind cause she wasn't studyin nothin but that courthouse and that magnolia tree.

By Sunday, everybody was talkin bout her and wonderin why she kept on standin in the middle of town lookin at the courthouse. Then Reverend Darden started preachin gainst worryin bout other folks's business and not takin care of your own, so I started feelin shamed. But deep inside I was still wonderin bout Mavis. I decided I was gonna walk up to Mavis and find out what she was up to.

Next day, I got up early, went to town, and walked right up and waited for her to say somethin. But she acted like she didn't even know I was there. So I started talkin bout the weather, bout how that old sun was beatin down on us today, and wasn't it somethin how the grass stayed green in all this heat? Then I commenced to fannin myself, but Mavis still didn't say a word.

I was standin there fannin for bout five minutes when Mavis turned them yella eyes on me. Now, I heard stories bout people talkin with they eyes and never even openin they mouths, but I never met nobody like that before.

Mavis had them kinda eyes and she put em on me and told me with them eyes that she come for somethin she lost, then she turned her head back round and fixed her eyes on that courthouse again. Well, it was plain to me she wasn't gonna say no more, and I was ready to go home and sit in some shade anyway, so I did.

That evenin when Tad come by for a visit, he was all in a uproar.

"Why you messin round with that woman?" he ask after I told him I'd stood up at the statue with Mavis for awhile. "I told you that woman sound like trouble. Folks say she rode off with that old Ned Crowell yesterday evenin and he ain't been heard from since."

"Where she at?" I asked. For some strange reason I was scared for her.

"She still standin up there like she always do. Layin back on that old statue. Somethin wrong with that woman. I told you the first time you told me bout her. Somethin wrong. You best stay away from her fore you get tangled up in some mess you be sorry bout. You know how them folks be."

"Don't go and get so upset your blood goes up, Tad. Ain't nothin gonna happen round here."

I tried to make Tad loosen up and grin a little, but he was too worked up and decided he was goin home to rest. I wasn't gonna tell him bout Mavis and her talkin eyes cause he'da probably thought I was losin my mind.

I let three days pass fore I went to town to see if Mavis was still standin at that statue, and sure enough, there she was.

I went and stood next to her and started talkin bout nothin in particular. I fixed my eyes on the courthouse but couldn't see nothin that hadn't been there for at least fifty years.

"You know they keep that buildin pretty clean and old Wonzell Fitch picks up round the yard every evenin. You might wanna check with him bout findin somethin you lost," I whispered.

She turned her head and told me with them yella eyes she was lookin for somethin that b'longed to her. She didn't even hear what I said. I didn't say nothin else, just stood with her for awhile, then went on home.

Tad came by later on with his face all wrinkled up like a prune, but I didn't make fun of him cause I could see he was troubled.

"Seem like three more of them Crowells and one of them Fitzhughs is gone."

"Don't nobody know what happened to em?" I asked. "Don't seem possible four grown men could disappear without a trace. What do folks think is happenin?"

"Don't know for sure, but some folks say they saw least two of them Crowells and old Billy Fitzhugh go off with that crazy woman late in the evenin."

"Do the sheriff know bout that?" I asked.

"Naw, and ain't nobody gonna tell him neither. If they do they likely to get locked up."

"Well, sure is mighty strange. Didn't think she even left that spot at the statue to go relieve herself. She just stand there starin, don't ever see her drink no water or nothin, just standin in all that heat."

"Well, look like come evenin she find herself one of

23

them old white men and go off with em and don't nobody see that man no more. You ain't goin round her, is you? I sure hate to see what happen when the sheriff find out bout her bein the last one seen with them missin men, cause you know well as I do what that mean."

Me and Tad just sat together real quiet and still on the porch holdin hands like old folks is supposed to do.

Next day I had to take Aunt Myrtice to evenin prayer service so I decided I was gonna sit outside and watch the statue from the front steps of the church.

"You bout to miss service and then have the nerve to sit on the front steps of Reverend Darden's church?" she fussed.

"I'm gonna do just that and ain't nobody gonna stop me, neither."

"You gonna sit outside when you need to be inside?"

"Yep," I replied. Then I just stopped listenin. I already made up my mind bout what I was gonna do, and even Aunt Myrtice's fussin wasn't gonna change that.

So after all the folks had gone inside, I sat on the porch and watched the sun go down and watched Mavis standin at the statue lookin at that same buildin she'd been lookin at for almost a month now.

When the shadows had stretched and twisted into night, I saw the lights from some kinda car stop in front of the statue. Mavis jumped in the car with what sounded to me like a laugh, and the car eased on down the street.

"No tellin where they goin," I thought out loud as the car moved slowly past the church. I could see the pale face of old Doc Adams at the wheel. Mavis never even turned her head in my direction or anyone else's. Her yella eyes was lookin straight ahead.

▼▲▼▲▼

"Nuther man gone," Tad mumbled when he stopped by the next day.

"Was it old Doc Adams?" I asked, scared to hear the answer.

"How'd you know? I done told you you better stay way from that woman. God knows what she's up to and I sure don't want no parts of it. You askin for trouble, Lady, foolin round that woman. Best go on in the house and read some of that Good Book you always talkin bout. I know it don't say nothin good bout killin folks!"

"Now how you know anybody been killed, Tad? How you know that? Some folks is just missin, right? Don't nobody know where they at, right?"

"You don't have to be no schoolteacher to see what's happenin! Them men be dead. Just as sure as we sittin here, they dead! Now you better stick round home with Miss Myrtice cause this town gonna turn upside down when they go after that woman!"

That night I turned over in my mind what Tad had said. Could Mavis have killed all them men? How could she do it? She ain't even a big woman. How could she kill even one grown man, even if he was old? And why wasn't the sheriff doin somethin bout it? Couldn't he see Mavis standin right in the middle of town leanin on that statue, like we see her every day?

I could feel pressure buildin up in my stomach, a kinda tight boilin feelin I always got when somethin big was bout to happen. So I decided I best go up to town and tell Mavis to be careful cause folks was sayin and thinkin some pretty nasty things bout her. Not cause of the way she was dressed, but cause of her bein seen ridin off with all them white men and ain't nobody seen em since.

Well, there she was standin in her usual spot with her

eyes burnin holes in the courthouse. I didn't have time to mince words, so I didn't.

"Folks is talkin, Mavis. Talkin real bad bout you. Sayin crazy things like you tied up with the missin of some men round here and how you up to no good here in Brownville."

Mavis didn't say a word, just kept on lookin.

"This town'll surprise you. You might be thinkin we ain't nothin but backwoods, country-talkin folks, but we got as much sense as anybody else walkin round on two legs. And don't too many people sit up and talk this bad bout somebody they'd never even laid eyes on a month ago without some kinda reason and some pretty strong thinkin on it. Now I don't wanna meddle in your business none, but I think you got a right to know folks is callin you a murderer."

Mavis turned them yella eyes on me for so long I thought I might start smokin and catch afire. I mean, she burned me with them eyes: "I come for what is mine, somethin that belong to me, and don't none of y'all got a right to get in my way."

I stepped back from her cause she was lookin pretty fierce with them eyes of hers alight, but I still reached out to touch her arm.

"I just hate to see bad things happen to folks is all. I don't mean no harm."

And I turned to walk away. But it felt like a steel band grabbed my arm and turned me back round to look at them yella eyes: "Now you listen, listen real good cause I want all of y'all to know why I was here after I'm gone and I'm not leavin till my work is done.

"Way back when, I lived on what was called Old Robinson Road. Wasn't much to look at, but we had us a little place, a little land, some chickens and hogs. We growed most of our own food right there on our land and didn't hafta go off sellin ourselves to nobody. Not nobody, you hear me? We was free people: livin our lives, not botherin nobody, not messin in nobody's business, didn't even leave the place to go to church. We just lived on our land and was happy.

"Now some folks right here in this town got the notion in they heads that colored folk don't need to be livin on they own land, specially if it was land any white man wanted.

"Old Andy Crowell, who looks like the devil musta spit him out, got it in his head he was gonna take our land. Well, I don't know if they still makin men like they made mine, but my man knew and I knew wasn't nobody gonna get this land, not while we was standin and drawin breath.

"So we took to sleepin with a shotgun next to the bed and one by the front door, and my man even carried a little gun in his belt when he was out in the fields. I kept one strapped to my leg up under my dress.

"We went into the courthouse right here, and tried to find out bout the law, cause we knew had to be a law to protect us, one for the protection of colored folks seein as how slavery had been over and warn't no more slaves we knew bout.

"We went up to that buildin and s'plained to a man what call hisself a clerk that we had a paper tellin us to clear off our land. My man had the deed to that land cause he got it from his daddy who got it some kinda way durin slavery time, and nobody bothered him bout it cause he didn't let nobody know he had it.

"But it was his and we had the paper to show it, and

that ratfaced gopher callin hisself a clerk looked at the deed to our land—our land I'm tellin you—and that clerk took the deed to our land and crumbled it up and threw it on the floor and told us to get outta his office.

"My man was just lookin right in that clerk's face. Wasn't flinchin. Wasn't blinkin. Just lookin. But his eyes, oh his eyes was tellin that man a story, a story that old fool didn't even know he knew. And my man told that clerk all about it, and I picked up the deed to our land and we left.

"Well, it wasn't long after we'd gone to the courthouse fore they come for him.

"You know how they do.

"Sit up and drink a buncha liquor to give em guts they don't have, then they posse up and come ridin for you soon as the sun go down.

"You know who it is when you hear all them horses on the road. Then you look through the window and see them little flickers of light comin closer and closer, growin bigger and bigger till it looks like the sun's come gallopin down the road. Then they all in your yard holdin up they torches till the yard's lit up like daylight, but you know it's the devil's own night. You can smell him out in the yard all tangled up with flint and sweat and liquor. I know the stink of evil anywhere. Then my man picks up his gun and steps out into that red night and tells em to get off his land or he'll shoot. I could see the claws of the devil pullin on my man and I tried to pull him back to the house, but he pushed me back inside and his eyes told me how he loved me like he did his own life. Then the devil's fingers snatched him and his tongue wrapped round my man's arms and drug him out into the middle of satan's circle, where they all had white handkerchiefs knotted round they faces from they red eyes to they pointed chins.

Then they knocked my man down with his own shot-gun and they kicked him, each one takin a turn. I picked up the shotgun standin near our bed and ran out the house screamin and fired a shot. Two of em fell to the ground, but some of em grabbed me from behind and beat me in the head. By the time I opened my eyes, my man was gone. It was Edith Rattray who come round and found me lyin in the yard and cleaned me up and nursed me. I musta laid in bed for over a month fore I could get up and go to town and find out what happened to my man.

"And what I found out was this: Evil can grow up outta the ground just like a tree filled with bad sap and turn every livin thing to somethin rottin in the sun like an old carcass.

"Now, you tell them folks what's wonderin why I'm here and what I'm doin and what I'm up to, you tell em that I'm cleanin that tree right down to the root."

Sayin that seemed to make that cold steel band slip from my arm. Mavis turned her eyes back on the court-house.

▼▲▼▲▼

I sat on the porch even though it was in the middle of the noonday sun and thought about what Mavis' eyes had told me.

"I must be losin my mind," I said to the listenin trees.

How in the world could a woman tell me any kinda story with no sound comin outta her mouth? What kinda woman was she? And what kinda woman am I? And what would God say bout all of this? I went inside the house and reached for my Bible. Surely some kind of answer could be found there.

After readin a while, I still hadn't found the answer I was lookin for, so I went into the kitchen and started cookin instead.

"What's for supper, daughter?" Aunt Myrtice asked.

"Oh, I'm fixin some squash, some fried catfish, some salt pork, a pot of blackeye peas, a pan of cornbread, and some peach cobbler for dessert."

"Um um. Tad must be comin by. I know you ain't fixin all that food for just me and you."

"Yeah, Tad did say he was comin round here later this evenin. Maybe I'll take you up to prayer meetin fore he gets here."

"Umhum. Y'all gonna get me outta the way so you can sit in this house kissin while I'm gone. You oughtta be shamed of yourself, old as you is."

"I might be gettin on in years, Aunt Myrtice, but I ain't dead yet." I kept on cookin.

I decided I was gonna get Tad to help me watch and see what Mavis was up to that evenin after we dropped Aunt Myrtice off at the church.

"You want me to do what?" Tad shouted after I told him what I wanted. "I ain't goin nowhere near that woman and you ain't either. You wanna get us both killed?"

I patted his arm and talked to him soft as I could to try to calm him down. No sense in his blood goin up over this foolishness.

"Tad, I just wanna prove to you and everybody else that Mavis ain't killed nobody and she ain't done none of us no harm by standin up by that statue. She can't even talk, how she gonna kill a big, old man?"

Tad gave in even though I could see he didn't wanna. He parked the car bout a block away from the statue. We didn't worry bout whether or not Mavis could see us cause she wasn't lookin at nothin else but that tree in front of the courthouse.

"Now look at her. You know somethin wrong," Tad said.

"Don't go and start workin yourself up. We ain't gonna be here long cause it's already startin to get dark and you said she usually leaves bout this time, didn't you?"

"I don't know when she leaves, cause I ain't been round here to see it. Folks just been sayin she leaves bout this time."

"Well, we'll wait a little while and see."

Sure enough, fore too long, an old red pickup pulled up next to Mavis and she ran around the front of the truck and jumped inside.

Even from where we was parked we could hear the sound she made when she got in the car. It wasn't no laugh, like Tad said, it was more like a high-pitched cryin sound mixed up with a whoop and a holler. It made the hair on the back of my neck stand straight up, and Tad said it made his flesh crawl.

Anyway, the truck pulled off and we followed a ways behind it. Couldn't see who was drivin on accounta that big old rebel flag hangin up in the back window.

We followed em anyway: out past the old poorhouse, past the pea and okra shed, past the old Lee plantation, out past Old Robinson Road.

Tad started gettin mad again cause he wanted to turn round and go back home. "You know we goin too far from home. Ain't no tellin where that crazy woman goin."

"Hush, and keep drivin. We gonna prove somethin once and for all tonight. Put a end to all this talk bout murder."

So we kept on drivin, but it was so dark now, we couldn't really make out what we was passin.

After a while, Tad said, "I don't think we in Brownville no more. You can tell by the shape things make in the dark."

I didn't say nothin. Just kept my eyes on the truck's red lights in front of us. A few minutes later, the truck pulled off the road and went into the trees. When we reached the spot where they turned off, we couldn't see no road, no lights, no nothin. Just trees.

"Well, I guess this is far as we go. Ain't nowhere to go now but back home," Tad said. "They probably went back up in them woods to do they dirty business."

"What dirty business, Tad? What dirty business? First you callin her a murderer, now what you callin her?"

"What kinda woman drive off with men in trucks in the evenin? What you think I'm callin her?"

"Let's just walk a ways in there to see if we can hear somethin."

"I'm not walkin back up in them woods. Now you go on and walk up in there if you want to, I ain't goin nowhere but back home."

While we was fussin, a car pulled off the road next to Tad's car. A skinny-faced man leaned out the window.

"You folks havin trouble?" he asked.

"I musta made a wrong turn somewhere back down the road and we just tryin to figure out the best way to get back home," Tad replied.

"You sure musta made a wrong turn cause ain't nothin out this way but trees and swamp."

"Is that right?" Tad asked.

"Yep, that's right. That big old yella swamp is bout two miles in them trees and it ain't nowhere no human man or woman needs to go. Ain't nothin livin that went in that swamp ever come back out that way. Nothin but the shadows of death back up in there. You step through them trees and it's like you stepped down into a tunnel goin way down into the ground. Down there them old snakes hangin down from them trees like moss is yella. Mosquito bites turn a man's blood yella. Yella flies crawl on the ground where worms come up out the yella mud and twist like broken fingers from a hand. Shadows come up and wrap they arms round you, pullin you down into yella mud where sounds don't come from this world. Nothin down there but yella."

Me and Tad thanked the man and turned the car around and went back home. The skinny-faced man's words burned our ears.

"Now don't you try to get me to run round on no wild goose chase behind that woman no more. I don't care what she's up to, I don't want nothin else to do with her."

Next day first thing, I went to town to talk to Mavis. Sure enough, there she was standin next to that statue.

"I been thinkin bout what you told me bout the evil way back when, and it seems it might be better just to let things lay and forgive the ones that did it like Jesus would."

Well, what did I go and say that for? Mavis whipped her head round and shook me with them eyes.

"Who you to forgive all that blood? Who YOU? Put your head to the ground and listen. Down there's an underground river runnin straight through this town, an underground river of blood runnin straight through. Just listen."

Then her eyes let me go and she turned back round. When I turned to walk back home, I saw some old dried-up mud caked round the bottom of that red dress she was wearin, mud that was yella as mustard, but dried up like old blood.

Not long after Mavis shook me up with them yella eyes of hers, I got sick and Aunt Myrtice, poor thing, had to tend me best she could, bless her heart.

Tad came by and helped when he could, but I'm the type of person don't like folks to see me hurtin and I sure didn't want Tad to keep seein me with my teeth out and my hair all over my head, though he claims I still look good to him.

Aunt Myrtice act like she don't hear him, but I could see her eyes light up.

Once I got to feelin better and was almost back on my feet, Tad started hunchin up his eyebrows, so I knew pretty soon we was gonna go out on the porch and get to arguin bout fornicatin, which to tell the truth, I'd rather be fussin over than that foolishness bout Mavis.

But Tad told me Mavis wasn't standin up at the statue of not-George Washington no more and nobody knows where she went off to. She just disappeared easy as she come.

The sheriff never did find out bout her. It turned out all them old missin men had been tangled up with the Ku Klux years back and had spilt plenty blood in the yard of that courthouse, hangin folks from that magnolia tree.

Sometimes, now, I think bout what Mavis told me how evil grow up outta the ground and how that old underground river flows with blood, and I think about puttin my head to the ground just so's I can listen. But I just go and stand by that statue and look up at that courthouse, feelin Mavis in my eyes.

FLOATING

I

1963

This a funny place. Maybe cause of the mountain standing up behind our town watching like a big old eye. Or maybe it's that lake stretching way out, reaching black to black, pushing its way cross the earth like it's in a hurry to run away from here. Or maybe it's that twisted-trunk, yellow-leaf tree next to Blue-the-wanga-man's house, with the leaves that shine like gold lamps through the trees, day or night.

But some folks say it's not that mountain sitting back watching over us, and it's not that black lake reaching, and it's not that old white-trunked, yellow-tipped tree next to Blue's that Reverend Daniles swears covers a hole leading from this world to the next. The thing that makes Pearl a funny kind of place is all that whispering we hear coming up from the ground.

I first heard it one day when I was walking with Miss Marius from her house to town.

Even though the only place I ever lived was in her house, I never thought of her house as mine. And don't nobody else think no different from me.

My mama left Pearl soon as I was born, back when the mine closed down and lots of colored folks left town.

But I remember when I was back in my mama's

stomach, floating like a pickle in a jar. I remember what was said, the bargains struck.

I could hear them talking while I was floating, sitting in all that water.

A high dark sound, my mama's laughing and crying, and a long, sharp tone, smooth and sharp as the knife Miss Marius used to cut meat from bone. I remember Miss Marius talking, talking, saying the same words over and over till my mama's cry turned into a stretched-out moan.

And Miss Marius going around in the water with me. Going around, swirling in the tart, dark liquid. The low sound of her voice stroking me inside that bag, inside that wineskin where I floated in a dream.

"What did you take, Nola? What did you put up inside yourself, child? Tell me. I'm gonna help you and I'm gonna help this baby, too, but you got to tell me what you put into yourself. I got most of the okra out, but what else? What was it, Nola? Was it something from inside the house, something from the woods?"

And Miss Marius and my mama went around, circling till my mama, exhausted, let the words fall from her lips like some hard, funny-shaped stones. "Cedar berries and camphor," she said, and that's all I remember from when I was in my mama's stomach. But folks don't know I even remember that, not even Miss Marius, cause them first years Miss Marius' deep voice and big-knuckled hands was all the mama I thought I'd need.

"Hush that foolishness, child," Miss Marius always say. "Everybody needs they mama and you got one just like everybody else. She'll be back when she gets a notion."

But it scared me when Miss Marius talk like that. I don't know if I like my mama's notions. The very first one she ever took about me left me shriveled up and gasping inside her womb.

That's why I come out looking so old and wrinkled everybody took to calling me Raisin. But I don't think it's the wrinkles that make me look old. I think it's like Miss Marius say, I'm an old old soul.

We live out on the edge of town on the east side where all the colored people live. Miss Marius' house is the last one you come to fore you hit all them trees and marsh at the edge of the lake, out where old Blue lives.

We live in what used to be an old rooming house. We got a downstairs and a front room and a kitchen with a big black stove. Upstairs is where we all sleep. Miss Marius and Nathan in the big room at the front of the house with that window letting in all the light from the world.

Miss Marius and Nathan got no children of they own, but Lucille and Lucinda act like they the ones come outta Miss Marius' body, even though Miss Marius say we all her children. Since they been here the longest, longer than my twelve years, they both get to sleep in that room big enough to be a play yard with all them goop-d-goos they got spread out all around the floor. They both got white-painted beds with flowers all scrolled around they heads so when they laying in em, it's like they laying inside a wreath, kind of like a halo around they heads.

I sleep with MC and Wilhemina and Douglass in the back bedroom in that big old brown bed that we climb up onto with a stool. It be tight sometimes with all us squeezed up in it, but I'm just glad I don't have to share the bed with Lucille.

Lucille gonna be big, just like Miss Marius. She got a thick-waisted body and short, strong legs. Her neck's thick, too, and strong enough for all the yelling she think she gotta do. She like to drop her head back and yell loud as she can. Her hair ain't black and thick like mine. It's the color of a tree trunk and her eyes the color of moonstone.

One time at supper I made the mistake of trying to tell her how pretty I thought her eyes was, but she raised herself up like a rattler in her chair and hissed, "Shut your mouth, you old wrinkled-up raisin, fore I put you in a box and sell you to Miss Lomax to eat."

Everybody at the table laugh when she say that. They scared not to. But Miss Marius and Nathan never crack a smile.

I didn't mind. Whenever they start talking about how wrinkled up and black I am, I just close my eyes and think of a warm soft place like a tub of hot water I can lay my body down in, or a nice dark space like a womb.

Lucille say don't nobody love MC, Wilhemina, Douglass, and me, and that's how come we living with Miss Marius and Nathan. MC ain't nothing but a baby so it always make him cry when she say that, but Wilhemina, Douglass, and me all about the same size, so we don't cry, we just look at her.

"Your mamas left you on Miss Marius' porch like a sack of bad-luck pennies. Ain't nobody ever gonna love you," she liked to say, knowing nobody try to talk about how her own mama left her.

When she say that I think of the time Douglass stuck his hand in a bucket of snakes and pull out three so I won't have to, like Lucille was trying to make me do. And Douglass about as scared of snakes as me.

Douglass' mama took all her children but him back to Memphis a while after the mine closed. She left him with Miss Marius so he'd be in good hands.

"That boy slow, Miss Marius. Look at the way that eye jumps, the way he rocks on his feet. He can't make it on this long trip. Can he stay with you till I get settled? I'll send for him soon as I do."

Miss Marius say, "I'll keep him till you ready, Louisa. Y'all go on and make your home."

Wilhemina's mama did her about the same as mine did me, cept she use a wire to try to get Wilhemina out.

"She a special child, Leona, that's why she here. Leave her with me. I'll take care of her," Miss Marius say.

Wilhemina got a mark look like a blue moon setting on her face. I think about how she sit with MC, humming in his ear soft as water the times he sound like there's a hole in him so deep nothing but water could fill it up.

I think about the way we sleep, four brown spoons with our arms around each other. And I look at Lucille when she say don't nobody love us.

I look at her mean as that goat Miss Marius call Moses on account of his white beard hanging down to the ground. I look at her mean as Moses look at us and I say, "No, you lying, Lucille. Somebody do love us."

And I don't even flinch when she grab me by the two plaits Miss Marius wove into my head. I don't even yell when she pull out the weave and swing me by my plaits to the ground.

I only remember the time I was over to Miss Lomax' house when she first got her new TV and out of the blue glowing in the screen I saw a cowboy jump out of a box and dig his heels into a horse's sides. The man jumped off the horse and grabbed a cow by the horns and tried to drag the cow down to the ground.

And when Lucille swung me down by my plaits into the dirt, just like that cowboy roped that cow, I jumped up with a wild-look still in my eyes and say, "You're still lying." But my legs were turning like wheels on the road.

II

This my secret place. My green, green holy place, inside this circle of red cedar trees, next to that big-leaf maple with moss that clings to it like smooth, green skin. Even the ground is green and covered with leaves, leaves my teacher Miss Dubois say is called oxalis. I put one of the leaves in my mouth and taste its juicy sour, then rub the green softness into my wrinkled skin.

"One day these wrinkles be gone and my skin be smooth and soft as these leaves. One day it will," I sing into the ears of licorice ferns and salmonberry. Then I lay down to dream on a wild ginger blanket, my smooth, soft second green skin.

A woman comes down the road toward me, a small black bag in one hand. Her eyes are knives and she is not smiling. Behind her is a bright gray cloud. It is raining white balls, but she is not wet. The woman's arms reach for me, brown and unwrinkled. She opens her mouth, but no sound comes out. I turn from her and run toward the black lake. The woman is behind me, running. She is fast, almost faster than me. I run to the edge of the lake, look back at her reaching hands, her mouth opened like an O. I jump. The water's coolness soothes me, then starts to burn. I call for help, but she is the only one there, standing, waiting at the edge. My head slips below the surface, I scream as I go down.

"Wake up, girl. What's wrong with you?"
I open my eyes and see Sin-Sin standing over me. He's the color of that stone Miss Dubois got on her desk,

Brazilian agate. His skin so bright it shines.

"What are you doing in my secret place, Sin-Sin?"

"This ain't your secret place," Sin-Sin say. "It ain't nobody's secret place cause it ain't even no secret. I walk around back here all the time. So does Blue."

"I never saw neither one of you down here before and I always come down here."

"Well, so do we. What you doing falling asleep out in the woods, girl? Don't you know all kinds of things be out here waiting on somebody like you?"

Sin-Sin ain't but fourteen, so I know he don't have to talk like I ain't got good sense.

"Ain't nothing out here waiting on me no more than it waiting on you. How come you walking around down here?" I ask.

"To get away from my mama," he say.

"What you want to get away from Miss Dubois for? She nice."

"That's cause she ain't your mama. She was, you'd be running down here hiding, too."

"I wish my mama was a schoolteacher," I say.

"That's cause you ain't never lived with a schoolteacher mama before, that's all. Once you get a taste of all the books she make you read, you be glad you got the mama you got."

"Miss Marius my mama."

"That right? I thought she Lucille and Lucinda's mama."

"She is. She our mama, too: me and Wilhemina and MC and Douglass. She our mama, too, sort of."

"Your mamas left all of you for Miss Marius to keep?" he ask.

"Uh huh," I say back.

"You're lucky. Mamas are hard on you, making you

work all the time around the house and read all the time and study figures and wash your hands before you come in the kitchen and they always wanting you to clean your ears. And they don't want you to talk like you want to talk. I wish mine would leave me with Miss Marius."

Then, it seem like every time I go to my secret place, Sin-Sin there. We run through the trees and play explore, picking up leaves and bugs and mushrooms.

We pull some big sticks and leaves together into something looking kind of like a shack, but Sin-Sin say it gonna be a tree house like he read about in a book his mama give him.

"We can't call it that, cause I ain't climbing up in them trees," I tell him so he can hurry up and get that thought out of his head. These trees around here big and tall, go back a long, long way, clear to what Miss Dubois call Lewis and Clark. He poke out his lips a bit, but we still don't put that house up in them trees.

We find two big rocks for chairs and a piece of log for a table. Most times we just sit inside and tell stories.

"Miss Marius say one time she saw the Night People down here," I say.

"What she say they look like?" Sin-Sin ask.

"Just like everybody say, tall as some of these trees, snake-haired and yellow-eyed," I say. "That's how she saw one cause its eyes was glowing in the dark and she thought it was a cat way up in the branches, but when she heard it whistle, she knew it wasn't no kind of cat."

"What was Miss Marius doing out in the woods at night? You can't see no Night People unless you out here at night," Sin-Sin say.

"She out here looking for Miss Buchanan."

"That lady walk around all the time talking to herself and stay out by the dump?"

"Miss Marius say that's how she got like she got. When they was girls they was friends and Miss Buchanan was alright then.

"But one day she got it in her head to run off to the woods cause her mama had died and her daddy wouldn't stop acting like he was crying all the time, even after her mama had been dead for a long time, and Miss Buchanan couldn't take it no more cause she thought her daddy would've liked it better if she was the one to go, which wasn't true, Miss Marius say, but the girl wasn't thinking right by then, so she took off.

"Miss Marius thought she knew about where Miss Buchanan had hid herself so she set off to go get her. Well, after she walked way up in here, she thought she'd gotten lost, which was strange for her cause she thought she knew these woods like the back of her hand, even in the dark.

"It was about then she looked up and seen them two shining yellow eyes in a tree. She thought it was a cat, but then she saw it shake its head side to side real slow and she saw them snakey ropes swing around. She couldn't make out no arms or legs, so she thought it must be sitting up in the tree.

"Then it turned them yellow eyes on a spot back of Miss Marius and start whistling. She say it don't sound like nothing from this world. She still don't move a muscle cause she think it might suck her up in them trees or something. So she stay still while she look in them eyes.

"She say it seem like something was being passed on to her while she was looking in them eyes, seem like she feel a humming in her body.

"Then she heard a moan coming from somewhere behind her. She turn her head to try to see exactly where the moan was coming from and then she heard a whirring sound and turn her head back to them eyes, but they was gone.

"She move over to the moaning and find Miss Buchanan laying on some moss. She didn't never say nothing that made sense no more."

"I bet they put a spell on her. That's what they supposed to do if they catch you out in they woods at night," Sin-Sin say.

"Miss Marius say she never did go back in them woods at night no more and she told us we better do the same."

"Well, all I know is, I'm not scared of no Night People whistling and carrying on," Sin-Sin say.

"What you gonna do if one sees you? Them people carry spears and can fly. What you gonna do if you come up against one of them?" I ask.

"Blue say Night People only bother people who bother them or theirs. He say they ain't nothing but old ones who've gone before us."

"What he mean?"

"He mean Night People ain't nothing but spirits."

"Ghosts?"

"No, spirits. People that are there, but we just can't see em. Blue say spirits around us all the time."

I look outside our house into the listening trees. I hear birds talking, leaves brushing up against each other. I look at Sin-Sin's eyes shining in the light and I know I ain't never gonna tell no more stories about Night People.

One time, I tell all the stories for about a week and Sin-Sin don't say too much of anything one way or the other.

I decide I ain't gonna tell another story till he take his turn. So, we pick more leaves and grass for our roof for a while and then come inside our house and sit down.

Sin-Sin wiggle for a while on his chair, but I still don't
say a mumbling word. He finally sit still and look at me
with a face that older than mine.

"The Night People come for me one time," he say and
wrap his skinny arms around hisself and start to rock his
body side to side like Douglass do.

"What you say?" I ask.

He close his eyes and I lean up close to his face to
hear.

"They come for me once and say they gonna come
back."

Sin-Sin look like I feel thinking about the Night People
coming anywhere for me.

"They come to your house?" I ask.

Sin-Sin nod his head, slow-like.

"Come right inside and got in my bed, climbed right
inside my head."

"Huh?"

"I was dreaming. I was standing near the edge of the
lake. Could hear the sound of water licking the rocks.
Could hold out my hand and touch the lumps on a white
stick laying on the bank like a long broken arm. The air
smelled like mud.

"It wasn't real. The waves was moving like a million
mouths opening their lips and talking. Talking to me.

"I stepped up, close to the edge as I could get without putting my feet in the water. The black water in that
lake turned orange as a rusty tangerine.

"I felt my daddy in there.

"I put one foot in the water and the talking mouths
pulled me in and I fell inside that water and floated in
the dream. Didn't hear nothing but whispers. The shushing
of the waves.

45

"Saw a shape drift by. Something tell me, that's him. That's my daddy. I follow the shape. Move my body in the water like it do. Something hold me. Something grab my arm, turn me around. Push something solid in my mouth. I swallow. My mouth taste like rock.

"I turn my head toward the shape I think is my daddy, but he gone. The mouths, the waves tell me to hush. They hold me by my arms and rock me. Sing me a song but I can't understand the words.

"I try to say, I want my daddy. I want to go with him, but they say no. Say it not my time. Say I will see him when my work is done. Then I will go where he goes, be what he is.

"I try to say no, but red wings fly toward me in the water. I feel a great bird grab hold of my shoulders and lift me. Then I am leaving the dream place, the dark orange water, the place where I felt my daddy.

"The bird take me up in the woods to a circle of tall, snake-haired trees.

"The trees whistle and open their arms. The bird drop me in the middle of their circle and fly away, red wings glowing in the dark.

"In their whistle-talk they tell me to climb inside the trunk of the oldest tree, say I should wait inside there until it was my time.

"I climb inside the white-walled hole and look out into the yellow-eyed night. Inside my head I call on my daddy.

"The trees keep whistling as they cover the hole and seal me inside the darkness."

Sin-Sin crying when he finish his story, long salty tears that move down his face leaving slug trails. The only boy I ever seen cry was MC and he ain't nothing but a baby. I don't know what to do with Sin-Sin's tears. So I pick up a leaf and smooth it on his face.

"It ain't nothing but a dreamstory, Sin-Sin, nothing but a dream," I say while I smooth the salt into his orange skin.

"I ain't never gonna know nothing about my daddy," he whisper.

He turn his head and look at me close.

"You ain't never gonna tell nobody, is you?"

"What I want to tell that for?" I ask back.

"You gotta promise," he say.

"Alright."

"No, I mean you really gotta promise. We gotta seal it with blood."

I look at him close and say, "I ain't sealing nothing with no blood."

"Alright. A kiss then. A soul-kiss," he say.

"What a soul kiss?" I ask.

"Here. I'll show you," he say.

Sin-Sin lean up against my face and put his lips against mine. I smell the green from the leaf in his face. It smell like green water. He push his tongue in my mouth. I start to bite, but don't. Sin-Sin taste like salt. He pull his tongue out like a snake sucking in.

"That's a soul-kiss," he say, not looking old no more. "That's as good as a bloodseal."

III

That the last time I see Sin-Sin in our treehouse for a while. I see him in school some time, but he turn his head like he don't wanta see me.

I try to tell him one more time I won't tell Miss Dubois

47

or nobody else. We could make a soul-kiss if he want. But he turn from me whenever he see me coming, like he turning from something evil in a dream.

I don't mind. I keep on going to my secret place, sitting inside the treehouse and telling stories to myself.

After a while, I stop worrying about Sin-Sin and his secrets cause Miss Marius got a note from a woman saying she my mama.

I bring it out here and puzzle over it sometime. Feel the loop-d-loop of Miss Marius' name on the paper and the other strange, dangerous name.

Dear Miss Marius,

Things sure do change, so do people. What goes around comes around in a hurry they say. I'm coming around there for my child.

Please accept these few dollars as my thanks. The words'll have to wait till I come.

Nola Barnett
1653 Cottage Grove South
Chicago, Illinois

Miss Marius say this my mama. And Nola Barnett say she coming here to get me.

That's when I first heard the whispers, the ones coming up from the ground.

Me and Miss Marius was walking to the depot for the woman that say she my mama. We pass by Miss Lomax' and see Mr. Lomax sitting with his fiddle between his knees on his porch.

"How y'all doin?" he ask.

"Fine, Mr. Lomax," we both say. "How you?"

Even Miss Marius call him Mr. Lomax. He long and skinny and like to fuss with Reverend Daniles. Like to call him a jack-leg preacher that keep messing with people's minds. When I ask Miss Marius what he talking about, she tell me to stay out grown folks' foolishness.

"Don't neither one of them know what they talking about," she always say and keep on doing what she be doing.

Miss Lomax say that fiddling belong to the devil, so she get a brand new TV to run so Mr. Lomax won't play. But he still do. Sit right up in the room and fiddle like it the end of the world, Miss Marius say. Even with that TV set on.

Miss Lomax act like she don't hear him, keep right on watching that blue light in the TV. Some nights you can hear them both, the TV and the fiddle going on into the night.

"I gots my fiddle back, so I'm alright," Mr. Lomax say as we pass.

"Somebody took your fiddle, Mr. Lomax?" Miss Marius ask.

"Somebody tried to take it, but I'm too old and smart for that," he laugh as we walk on down the road.

When we on the stretch of road between Miss Lomax' and Miss Dubois', I hear them.

"What's that?" I ask Miss Marius, who keep on walking down the road.

"What's what?" she ask, still walking.

I stop dead in the middle of the road and listen, "You hear that?"

"I don't hear nothing but my heart beating in my ears from all this walking," she say. "You better hurry up. We don't want to keep your mama waiting."

I don't tell her I wait. All my life and I don't even know I'm waiting. Don't say, let her wait, let her sit there and think about things like I do.

But I keep hearing the sound. It start to build in my ears till I almost scream, but I don't. Miss Marius'd think I don't want to go see Miss Nola that say she my mama.

I don't want to go see her, but it's the whispers that stop me from moving.

The whispers jump up from the ground and settle in my bones until my body gets heavy like a big piece of wood and I'm stuck. My legs take root and I stand in the road with my arms stuck out.

The whispers move in them, too, a humming in my bones that circles around my waist tight as a belt and I can't breathe, can't move, can't even open my mouth to call out to Miss Marius.

The whispers sound like white-capped water swirling around inside my head till I think I'm gonna fall from the weight, but I don't.

The whispers hold me still and fill up my head with an old watery sound.....

WHOOSHBEE.....WHOOSHBEE.....WHOOSHBEE.....WHOOSHBEE

And I'm floating out there on that road, floating toward my mama.

"Floating" is an excerpt from the novel *One Dark Body*.

BigWater

It was almost time to go there. Keta felt it in her bones. Water coming down and her twelve-year-old frame filling and rounding. Water pushing past her lungs when she laid on her back in her skinny wooden bed, pushing past and up until her soft brown skin formed small rounded hills on her chest.

Keta tried to make herself small, tried to hide the secret of her body's slow unfolding.

"Stop hunching your shoulders, girl."

"Let us get a good look at you."

"Where'd you get those skinny legs?"

Her aunts' smiling litany of questions made Keta blink her eyes and drop her head.

These were the women—the overflowing thighs and hips of Aunt Sarah, the softening belly of Aunt Ruth, Aunt Ethel's branchlike limbs, the proud, wise head of Aunt Josephine. Keta would look at the bodies of these women when they gathered every Wednesday to sit in a circle in the early evening light on straight-backed chairs in her mother's living room.

She would stare at the abundant swells of her mother's warm flesh and then feel the two small lumps on her chest and say, "I'm never going to look like that."

"You have to start somewhere," Aunt Sarah would smile.

"You have plenty of time to grow, girl."

Aunt Ethel would hide her smile behind her hands and say, "Mine never did grow."

"They're not what make you a woman," Aunt Ruth would snort. Then, cigarettes in place, they'd all turn, clicking their heads back into their secret dark circle.

Keta looked at the shapes and sizes of the women as they laughed and fussed over grown-woman things. She stood at the edge of their laughter, a long black wire, wondering, what does it take to make a real woman?

BigWater. Her mother had gone there. And Aunt Ethel. And Aunt Ruth and Sarah. And Aunt Josephine forced to go, physically forced against her protests.

"It's coming."

"It's coming. She's almost there."

"Doesn't make any sense. Taking me out to that water. Doesn't make any sense."

In the end, though, even Aunt Josephine had gone: out past the edge of town, past a hundred miles of whispering trees, deep into the forest where old stones hold secrets, past walls of chiseled granite, over a silver ribbon bridge into mountains rising like indigo breasts, moving up, into air so blue your bones fill with light.

BigWater. Her mother had gone, and her mother's mother, and her mother before her, and all the way back to the very first. And soon, very soon it would be Keta's turn to listen to the old words of the women.

In the old before time, before the people's spirits were broken, before the many tongues were lost, before the ceremonies were hidden from those who would not

*understand, women bled together. The moon called out
to the water in their bodies, and they bled. One simul-
taneous stream of blood that carried them from world
to world. They were one flesh. One blood. One Mother.
The women left the nonbleeding girls, the boys and men,
and went into the menstrual huts to wash the moon.*

Then one morning, Keta woke to golden light filtering
through the curtains, her body slashed with yellow light
from her toes to the braids that lay across her head.

It had started as a seed of water planted deep within her
brain. With the whisper of a roar, it grew into a stream
soaring through her body toward her pubis, moving
straight to the heart of her womb where it circled, a liquid
burning star, before rushing toward the mouth between
her legs. First it paused, then pushed past the brown girlish
lips and flowed freely, a soft, strong, shining red river.

BigWater. Keta spent the first hours in bed with thick
cotton pads clenched between her legs tight as Aunt
Ruth's lips on her menthol cigarettes. She didn't know
when the women were coming, but she knew they were all
going to come. It was time.

Keta's mother entered a room made new.

"I knew it," her mother said, glancing at Keta's face. "I
knew it soon as I smelled that new woman smell, drifting
down the steps like clouds. You feeling alright?" she asked.

Keta nodded. "Feel alright, but kind of funny."

"That's natural. You're changing, baby. Changing from
one kind of being into another," her mother said as she
rubbed Keta's stomach with lavender oil.

The day after her bleeding stopped, the women brought
gifts to Keta's room.

Keta fingered a satin brassiere, a bottle of lavender oil,

a photograph of her great-grandmother, a gold robe. She stroked her grandmother's collection of sacred writings.

"Tonight we're going to take you."

"Don't be afraid."

"You're growing up."

"Now, you're one of us."

Aunt Josephine put her hands on Keta's stomach and said, "The blood is the line, Keta. The line passing through all of us. The ceremony marks the line, so you know how special it is. I thought I could be a woman without all that. But I didn't know what being a woman was. I didn't know about the power and the responsibility, until BigWater."

Keta was a bit afraid. Her mother leaned forward, brushing Keta's face with her lips.

"It's important what you are and what you're going to be. I want you to know that I'm proud."

"But I didn't do nothing."

"You're you, aren't you?"

"Yeah, but...."

"That's enough for me," her mother said and each woman hugged Keta fiercely.

As Keta lay in bed she felt herself grow big and small, light and dark, up and down. The blood had changed her, but she didn't know how. When would her breasts start to grow, when would her hips widen? Was she really now a woman?

"Here, drink this," her mother said, holding a cup of black liquid to Keta's lips. "You have to sleep until we get there."

Keta frowned as the warmth moved down her throat.

"We'll get you ready," Keta heard the women say as she began to float inside a deep black silence, warm as her mother's embrace.

"BigWater," breathed Aunt Sarah.

"It seems a hundred years since we've been here," Aunt Josephine said.

"Speak for yourself," growled Aunt Ruth.

"Are you ready?" Keta's mother asked.

Keta nodded, shaking herself fully awake. Her mother squeezed her hand.

"It's time," she said, pulling Keta from the car. "Watch out for the robe."

Keta stroked the softness of the golden robe while her mother covered her head with its hood.

"Queen Mother for a day."

"For an evening."

"For the rest of your life, if that's what you choose."

The sun left an orange light in the sky as shadows twisted and stretched across the ground.

"Do we have everything?" Aunt Josephine asked after they walked a short way into the trees.

Each woman stopped until they formed a dark knot in the path.

"Of course I know we have everything," Josephine said as she started the line moving toward the clearing once again.

Soon, they stepped from the darkness of the trees onto rocks shining like a skin holding water. BigWater, spreading before the women now, a sheet of shimmering blue-green glass.

"There it is, there's the one," Aunt Sarah cried as she pointed to the broad granite stone sitting in the center of a nest of white rocks.

"Here's where we walk."

"Careful, it's slick."

And the group moved slowly into the water across small

dark rocks. The women led the way and behind dipped Keta, the hem of the robe floating on the water like a soft yellow flower.

"This is it. This is the one," Aunt Sarah whispered as she sat on the smooth-skinned rock. The others sat too, in a tight dark ring around Keta.

Her mother opened the basket and removed five yellow candles, a cup of white ashes, a spoonful of honey, a packet of bitterroot, a bottle of wine, and a large carved wooden cup.

When the moon's white eye began shining through the trees, Aunt Sarah said, "Let's begin."

Josephine started to hum, an old sound each of the others in turn pushed into the circle until it melted into one long hum rolling over the water.

Keta's mother began:

"This is the place where we come to be women. This is the place we come to be whole. We are following the line of our mothers and their mothers back to the very first one. When the first blood comes and a mother's house fills with its heavy, warm scent, it is time. Are you ready to follow the path of your mothers?"

Keta nodded, though she didn't know yet what her mother meant.

"Don't be afraid, we're going to show you," Aunt Josephine soothed.

The women removed their shoes and eased their bare feet into the water. Then Keta was surrounded by a ring of heavy laughter that held her in a wild embrace before lifting into the air.

Her mother dipped her fingers into the cup of ashes and lightly brushed Keta's face with the soft white powder.

"The bones of the dead. Now you wear the mask of your

ancestors, the women who have gone before you and the women yet to come.

"Open your mouth."

Slowly, Keta complied. Her mother placed a drop of the root's bitter, milky sap on the left side of Keta's tongue and a drop of honey on the right.

"One side for the bitterness, one side for the sweetness of Life. Even your body will allow you goodness and sadness. To be a woman means knowing there are two sides to Life."

This was how Keta had felt when she became blood sisters, with her best friend Johnna. They had slit their fingertips with a paring knife, then mixed their blood. She felt safe now, in this circle of women.

"Be still and learn to listen to your body," her mother advised, as her aunts rose from the circle and laughed as they ran barefoot toward the lake's shore. They quickly returned, their long skirts dragging in the water.

"Eat the clay from their hands," her mother said. Each aunt presented a palm holding red clay to Keta.

"Our First Mother's blood poured from the moon into this clay. Her body is in this clay. We take Her body into our bodies so we will gain Her power, Her wisdom. We come here to eat this clay, to be still, to listen to our bodies' prayers. Smell the clay."

Aunt Sarah held the clay to Keta's nose. It smelled like wet dirt.

"This is the smell of our monthly blood, our blood that comes from the moon. People are made of moon-blood and clay. The spirits of our people flow in our blood. It is the blood of Life."

Keta ate some clay from each of her aunts' hands. The women also ate the clay.

"Take off your robe," Keta's mother instructed. Keta removed her robe and handed it to her mother. The women smeared Keta's body with the red clay.

Her mother's fingers gripped the slim bottle of wine and filled the wooden cup.

"This wine is the red water flowing inside you, the liquid cord winding from the women before us, through me to you, connecting us all to our First Mother, the source of all living things. This bloodwine is Her power, now yours. We will all drink from this cup. My mother told me this cup was carved by her mother's mother when she was a girl. You take the first sip, daughter."

Keta held the cup in both hands and raised it to her lips. She dipped her tongue into the pungent red liquid and smiled. This was her first taste of wine. It filled her head with a swirling watery glow.

"We are going to wash you after your first moon," her mother said. "For the last time, you will be bathed as a child. From now on, you will bathe as a woman and will be responsible for your own body."

Keta placed her bare feet in the water. Naked, she stepped from rock to rock as her aunts sat on the old stone laughing, water lapping at the hems of their skirts.

"Always remember how your body feels tonight. This is what happened to me and my mother and her mother before her," her mother said.

Keta watched her mother pass the candles to her aunts. As if looking through water, she saw her mother strike a match. Then Keta felt herself moving, her bones shifting, the candles' glow a fire inside her. She felt something more ancient than memory move through her blood as she moved among the smooth-skinned rocks.

Aunt Ethel leaned forward into the light of her candle

and took Keta's right arm. "We're going to wash you like we wash the sacred stones of our dead. We wash them so we can bring them back again, as you will come back. When you were born, the moon was white and had stood up again. It was your beginning."

Keta moved through the water and gave her left arm to Aunt Josephine, who leaned forward, face dancing in the candle's narrow flame. She rubbed the silken water into Keta's arm. "Now the moon is yellow and turning, twisting and turning like a woman trying to get full of herself, trying to become herself, as you will become. It is another beginning."

Keta moved around the circle to Aunt Ruth and put her foot in Aunt Ruth's lap. Aunt Ruth set her glass of wine on the rock and then moved her face from the darkness into her candle's light. As she bathed Keta's foot she said, "Soon, the moon will be full and red. After loving, after battling, the moon will sit down like a woman who has arrived, a woman who belongs, like you will belong. That, too, will be a beginning."

Aunt Sarah grabbed Keta's left leg, let the water drip over her foot. She moved her candle close to Keta's face and looked into the girl's eyes until satisfied with what she saw, then she backed away and said, "This long body is life, girl. Nothing but life. And a woman holds all these moons, all these beginnings inside her body. When the moon is black, it is the dying moon."

Aunt Sarah pressed her fingertips to Keta's forehead, streaking her skin with clay.

"But when the moon is dying," Aunt Sarah continued, "the circle is only half-complete. We must die to be reborn, to complete the circle of Life. That is why we are washing you like we wash the stones to bring back our dead. One part of your life is dying, another being born."

Keta's mother stepped into the water with Keta. She splashed Keta's body, using her hands as cups to pour water over Keta's head, her shoulders, her breasts and buttocks. Keta smiled as the water cascaded over her skin. The water flowed over her body as it had flowed over her mother's body and her mother's before her.

"This will be the only time I will do this," her mother said, kneeling in front of Keta's gleaming body to wash her pubis.

Finally, Keta's mother held her candle to her daughter's face and said, "After tonight, you will be clothed in the knowledge of all these women. This is what makes you a woman. Every month now you'll be reborn and you'll hear a sound like WHOOSHWHOOSHWHOOSHWHOOSH WHOOSHWHOOSHWHOOSH flowing through the water in your body. It's the old sound of where we all come from."

BigWater. The women were unashamedly drenched with water and wine, and Keta could see the magnificent outlines of their bodies. They talked into the night, their voices inflating Keta's head with notions she had never known until she felt herself swelling, growing larger than the tall black trees, felt her body opening with the sound of words shifting inside water, the bitterroot and honey on her tongue turning to water, her body brimmed with WHOOSHWHOOSHWHOOSHWHOOSH, growing larger, her body rounding with sound, with the women's laughter, and she grew larger still, grew past old granite walls, over indigo mountains, and into the blue-black air so high her body filled with light and the ancient shimmering of water.

THE PINK DOLPHIN

"We do not breathe alone," Albertina Woods solemnly proclaimed. I sat at her feet, a conjurer's apprentice, squatting outside her paling two-room sea island house set in a small clearing surrounded by ancient oaks and cypresses dressed in silvery moss. The house gaped at the narrow dirt road and the rolling sea beyond. At the end of a honeysuckle and wild grape-lined path, a sagging three-step porch held both our weights.

I had waited all of my life for this moment.

I had traveled a staggered line leading to Albertina Woods after seven years of searching for that one particular, absolute truth, the one truth I would be able to set the rest of my life by.

I was certain Albertina Woods possessed knowledge of this truth. Inside my pants pocket, glowing like a soft burning light, the yellowed newsprint was folded into a careful square. That news article was the singular match, the flame leading me to this old woman, this broken-down porch.

"That was the most wonderful part, the most beautiful revelation," Albertina Woods continued, as if each word spoken were a seed planted in soft yielding earth. "Did you know this?" she asked. I shook my head slightly.

"Those newspaper people always overlook everything else I tell them. They just want to talk about the pink dolphin. But you make sure you get the story right," she said.

I nodded my head, giving her a small gift of reassurance as I bent over the yellow tablet I held in my trembling lap. She reached down and stroked my nervous hands. I looked into her eyes and felt no more fear.

Was it true what they said about Albertina Woods? She did not look like a woman who'd had innumerable lovers. She was tall at eighty-eight, strong-voiced with wrinkleless skin the color of palmetto berries, her laughter a strong dark wine.

Still, it was hard to imagine her rail-thin body as once bewitchingly seductive.

She turned her fading black eyes on me and grinned, retracted her full lips to reveal proud white teeth, her own. She slowly shifted her weight on the smooth planks of the porch until the fabric of her festival-colored dress pulled tight across her thighs. Albertina's hair covered her head in thin white strips. Her fingers were warm, sinuous.

"You think a witch cannot have lovers? You think an old woman like me has never known how to ride?"

I turned my face from her hot question, turned and stared at the flowers in her yard, their blossoms like large vermilion heads nodding in the slow southern breeze.

"All the time they came around me, begging: make me clean, help me get clean deep down in my soul, Albertina. They came inside this body, my praise house, with the hope that they'd wash themselves and be released."

She stopped for a moment. Her dress fell between her legs outlining her narrow thighs in sharp relief. I looked away from those thighs, those old once-powerful thighs.

She brushed my cheek with her moist fingers, sensing my discomfort.

"You will have to look at this power, daughter. Look at this power so your soul will be released."

Albertina looked at me and sighed.

"You came for the dolphin, didn't you? Like all the others."

"Some say you had one for a lover," I said, a question rising behind my eyes.

Albertina stared at me. She nodded her head as if she had made up her mind about something.

"I couldn't work with everybody. One man I refused went to Uncle Friday, the rootworker, and asked for a hand."

"A hand?" I asked.

"A hand, a charm. The man planted the hand under my porch. I never was able to find it. People stopped coming around me looking for comfort. That was all I ever gave. Comfort. I had to make my own hand to bury in the yard, to reverse the spell that had been placed on me. Still, no one would come. Not a solitary soul. Soon, I began to believe I was supposed to breathe alone. Thought breathing alone was the way it should be. Like you, daughter."

She paused and looked at my folded hands, as if blessing the tools in my lap: pencils, paper, pens, tools I used to reconstruct the lives of unknown others. Lives broken. Shadowed. Winged. I did not want to show her my scars, the deep broken parts of myself. They had said her eyes could reach into your soul and hear things. I curled my shoulders, pulled my body back into itself.

"Echoes," she said, her dark eyes scanning my body. "The echoes brought him to me."

"Him?" I asked.

"The dolphin you came to hear about."

So, the stories I had heard about Albertina Woods were true.

"The hand," Albertina continued. "The hand he buried under my porch brought my spirit down. Low down. He put the hand down and when I lay in my bed at night I could feel a snake crawling inside my belly, a great snake moving inside my bones. Something had grabbed my soul, grabbed my soul and crushed it into the ground. No one would come around. No one would have anything to do with me. I'm talking about loneliness now. A deep hurting kind of empty. You know what I mean?" she asked.

I thought about the luminous blue inside me, the great shimmering gap that had brought me here. I nodded my head.

"Before the hand, I was a big black red-winged bird. Nothing could hold me down. But when the hand got hold and the snake moved inside me, it seemed as if I couldn't do anything to get off the ground. My hair stood on my head like antennae to God."

I reached for Albertina's hand, her thin fingers fluttering inside her lap like fragile birds.

"A woman can die without touching. Without hugging. Without love. The hand told me to go into the water, into the liquid darkness. Into a blue so deep it was black."

She stood. I stood. I held her hand as she crept down the three sagging porch steps as if she were once again descending into that water, that wide-lipped sea waiting beyond.

"I touched the bottom. The bottom of that blue-black sea. Dragged my feet through mud slick as silk. Creatures wrapped their limbs around my legs, barnacles clung to my skin like crusty jewels. I was as low as I could possibly descend.

"Then I felt a sound coming. A sound moving inside my body like raindrops on a tin-roof, Click Click Click CLICKCLICKCLICKCLICK Click Click Click.

"I turned my head and looked into the obsidian eyes of the dolphin. He looked into my eyes, heard my breath rising, heard the struggle of my burning lungs. I saw blood coursing through his body beneath almost translucent skin. He had as many scars as we do, daughter. Scars from brushing against life. He brushed his body against mine. Took one of his fins and slowly rubbed my belly.

"I didn't want to breathe any more. I closed my eyes and felt the clicking enter my body. Click Click Click CLICKCLICKCLICKCLICK Click Click Click. It seemed as if the clicks were saying: Breathe. Slow. Like me.

"The dolphin rubbed my belly again. Low down. Deep down. Then he was inside my body alongside the clicks, moving, pulsing, breathing air into my lungs, the breath of Life, air he would blow through the crescent-shaped hole on his back once he reached the surface of this black sea.

"We became water, pink and black water, and we merged inside a voluptuous silence, then turned into one shining muscle of pleasure inside the undulating midnight sea.

"The dolphin's breath pushed the snake out of my body. His clicks washed away the power of the evil hand."

Albertina stopped her story and turned back toward the porch.

"Was that the only time with the dolphin, that one time in the water?" I asked. She looked at me and smiled.

"He visits my bed from time to time," she said.

"What is it like, then?" I asked.

Albertina Woods clasped me inside her birdlike arms. "It's like loving yourself," she said, holding me as the dolphin must have held her, slow, tight, sweet, until I felt, rather than heard, the sounds of multitudes breathing, the sounds of all living things breathing. And hope rose inside me like a silvery-skinned flower or a fish that has suddenly sprouted wings.

"You are never truly alone, you know. Here," she said, pressing me against her breasts which were not much larger than my own.

"Here," she said. "Breathe deep. Like this."

Spirit Talk

he only magnolia in Pearl stood like an eternally ripening queen in Viola's front yard on Sienna Street. The tree was centuries old when Viola and Basil first moved into the slim, droopy-porched house, and it had stretched its limbs across the wide road by the time Basil was taken from the house, four years twenty-seven weeks and three days later, leaving Viola wild-eyed and sweating, clutching a blond-haired, green-eyed toddler to her chest as she stood crying in the middle of the yard.

"He's in me, I tell you. Right here inside my head. Can't you just listen?" Basil screamed as he tried to break free of the two white-coated men and stood in the yard with his arms outstretched.

"Can't you see all this light in me?" he cried, kicking his legs and arching his back, forcing the two starched men to grasp his arms even tighter.

"Can't you see him? Can't you see him in me, baby?" His eyes begged Viola as the two men held their mouths in thin white lines and pulled.

Viola tucked her head into her daughter's soft curls as Basil was driven down the street, a cloud of whirling red dust trailing behind, while Viola's tears dissolved like all of their dreams into Reba's warm scalp.

▼▲▼▲▼

"Ain't you hot in that thing, girl? Must be over a hundred degrees today!"

Reba kept her eyes on the road as Viola eased next to her on the sagging porch. The tree's white-cupped flowers sweetly scented the heavy hot air, some blossoms yellowing on the ground.

Viola took a slug from a bottle of Jack Daniels. She wiped her mouth with the back of her hand. Reba caught the hard glint of the diamond on her mother's fair finger. Her blood-red nails gleamed as her slender fingers clasped the bottle.

"Looks like Dr. Feelgood, that Rafael, ain't comin by after all. Thought you said he'd be by at noon to walk you to the bus stop? Never did think he was up to no good. Any colored man lookin that white should've been runnin this one-horse town by now. Don't know what it is you think you see..." Viola muttered as she took another long pull on the bottle.

Faces of neighbors bold enough to walk the street in front of her house began to blur into one long procession.

"I needs to get outta this place, too. This street done gone to the dogs ever since that heifer Juanita Tillson moved up here. Bringin all them nasty South Carolina ways here, makin life miserable for decent folk."

Reba strained her neck to look for Rafael. She hoped he'd hurry, Viola was likely to pass out soon.

"Yeah. I needs to pack my bags and head on up to Memphis. Or maybe Atlanta. Should still be plenty opportunities for a fine-lookin woman. Lookin finer every day. So, I'm a little soft round the edges? I'm soft and tough as leather, soft on one side, tough on the other.

Like a real woman. Not like one of them plastic wind-up toys. Not like JUANITA TILLSON!" she shouted at the short, bow-legged man walking down the street.

"Some folk don't know a real woman from a worm. Hey, I might even dye my hair red and act like I'm from Mexico!"

Viola stood crookedly and walked into the front yard. She pulled at the billowing housedress she always wore after getting home from the bakery where she worked. Pulled the material tight against her softening body, the fullness of her pendulous breasts accentuated for any passerby to see.

"Ain't this still some fine stuff?" she asked the bottle of whiskey as she swung her wide hips, shuffling her feet in their flat slippers.

"How does that go? *La cucaracha, la cucaracha,*" she sang, swinging her hips in a crazy circle. After a few moments, she stopped and stared accusingly at Reba.

"You could come with me if you'd let go of your triflin ways and take off that damn wig!"

Reba burned her green eyes into Viola's black pupils. Viola was not yet drunk enough to ignore that look.

"I don't know how you turned out like you did. Lord knows, I did the best I could, with no help from your daddy. Always talkin bout doin this and tryin that."

She snorted. "Ain't nothin worse than a poor man with a dream."

Reba stood, looking past her mother into the street.

"Ain't no sense in tryin to run from the truth. I ain't gonna lie to you bout your daddy. And that Dr. Feelgood ain't no different neither. Makin out like he's gonna take you off to some big city. Like he knows what to do in one when he get there. Man can't even live up to his color in this town. How he gonna make it in some other place, draggin you behind?"

Reba picked up her two suitcases and started down the steps. She had hoped things wouldn't turn out like this. She wanted to remember Viola standing up straight and looking half-way dignified, not this woman twirling in the yard with her housedress hitched, dancing in a circle, singing to a whiskey bottle. She walked up to her mother and dropped the suitcases into the red dirt.

"Mama, things are gonna be alright. You watch. Now, I want you to take care of yourself and I'll write soon as we get settled."

Viola grabbed Reba and held her, the mother's body for a hot minute soft as water.

"Seem like I can't keep neither one of you in this house. That's all I wanted, all I ever asked for was this house. And your daddy never cared. Wasn't no house in the world big enough to hold his spirit. You know I loved him the best way I knew how, same as you. You know that?"

"Yeah, Mama. I know."

The two women held each other, the slight one bolstering the stouter. Viola tried to snatch Reba's wig from her head but Reba jerked away from her mother's hands.

"Girl, what kind of man would want a woman like you?"

Reba turned away from the sharp question in her mother's eyes and picked up her bags. She looked at the old shotgun house and up into the protective arms of the magnolia tree that had shared the secrets of her life. Then she looked into the glassy eyes of her mother and walked slowly across the yard.

Viola turned from Reba: from her retreating back, the closed door at the bottom of her eyes, the crooked smile that had always reminded her how the girl had more of her daddy in her than Viola'd ever cared to admit.

As she sensed the warmth of Reba moving farther down the wide red road away from the house that had been all they had ever called home, Viola felt a coolness seeping into her bones until her hands spread like frozen fans of grief before her, catching her as she fell.

▼▲▼▲▼

Reba's thoughts traveled past the streets she walked. Several wide women peered uneasily at her from behind their faded curtains. Reba could almost hear the sharp intakes of breath.

The wig had never bothered her as it had agitated other folks. She had been tired of all the stares in her direction whenever she walked around bald-headed, so she bought the wig.

It was jet-black and made out of animal hair. The tight curls covered her head like sheep's wool and she loved the crinkly feel of it in her fingers. She felt blessed while wearing the wig.

It was as close as she had ever come to looking like the regal African women she'd seen in her father's vibrant sketches. The ones Viola kept in an orange treasure chest set apart inside her bedroom closet. The deeply shadowed Nubian eyes had jumped straight from the canvas into her heart.

"Your daddy couldn't sleep for his dreams. All the time sittin at a table tryin to stroke colors on a page. Wasn't no place for a man like that in this world. Not then. I tried to tell him, tried to get him to buck up and fly right like the rest of us, with his feet on the ground. See this one?" Viola had held a fading sketch to the light.

"This was one of the first. He kept sayin somethin was pressin inside, somethin that wanted to bust right through his skin. Next thing I knew, he done this."

Viola had placed the delicate sketch of a proud young woman in Reba's hands. Reba could have been looking into a mirror.

"It's you, honey. He drew this fore we even knew you was comin."

Reba always felt an old stirring, a deep longing each time she looked at that sketch: the tight-curled mahogany-colored woman with the wide strong nose and heavy-lipped mouth. She'd often pretended she was the colored pencil her father held between his butterfly fingers so lovingly he could make lines on a page look as if they were singing.

"He couldn't even sleep for his dreams," Viola mumbled after dropping the lid on the chest and hurriedly brushing past Reba to find her bottle, her friend.

Viola had tried with all of the strength and determination of her own portions of white blood to erase from Reba's mind any memory of Basil's talk about the glorious African past.

"Always talkin foolishness to that child and her not even old enough to understand it for what it is: just plain foolishness."

Reba had heard Viola mutter to herself on numerous drunken occasions: "She ain't no African, don't even look colored. What he want to make her life harder for?"

But Reba had tried to place herself in every one of her father's paintings, though she never felt her father had meant for his African queens to have blond hair.

Viola had almost fainted when Reba cut her blond locks.

"Have you lost your mind? Where is your hair?" she had asked before breaking down and crying. It had always been her pride she had given birth to a green-eyed, blond-haired girl.

"No one would ever guess your daddy's as black as a shadow under that magnolia tree," she'd tell Reba while lovingly fingering her hair. It was the only time Viola would touch her, to stroke her like a prized pony.

Reba had learned to thrive in spite of those strokes that pulled her away from anything African. That had been the beginning of Viola's days blurred by whiskey. Although she knew Reba did not listen to her ravings, the liquor spurred her on.

"You could have been SOMEBODY! Could've had the finest man this state has to offer. Don't you know you don't even look like you colored? I can't even walk down the street and hold my head up. First you bald as an egg, and now you got that damn nappy-headed wig! What's wrong with you, girl?"

Reba kept her head stiff and her eyes straight ahead.

"You know what folks is sayin, don't you? They sayin you done turned out just like your daddy! All I know is you keep this stuff up and you gonna end up in the same place he did!"

▼▲▼▲▼

Something long-rooted and old had been planted inside Reba way back before she had even come into this world. And as each year passed, the thing grew inside her until she felt she couldn't keep living in her old skin without shedding it and getting a new one. And all of the snooping questions and stale whispers about her and Viola and her daddy only seemed to help the thing grow inside her head.

"What are you?" pried the hawk-nosed teacher who

noticed neither black children nor the poor whites would ever play with Reba.

"What are you?" asked the brittle shopkeeper when Reba tried to buy a slinky red blues-singing woman's dress.

"What are you?" questioned the thick-jawed ebony girl as she grabbed Reba by her blond braids and swung her into the mud while the other children, black and white, stood around, laughing.

"What are you?" she'd ask herself as she looked into the mirror while marking her reflection with her mother's brightest lipsticks.

"What are you?"

▼▲▼▲▼

The tangy smell of seawater filled her nostrils as she walked through Pearl to the bus stop. Soon, she reached the market where she had worked for the past five years.

She would miss the sharp sea smells that always reminded her of the ocean, the brightly colored flesh of vegetables, the shimmers and shouts of the merchants.

The people at the market knew to leave her alone. She would go into her stall and spread her goods on the table: necklaces made of polished stones she'd found while walking near the river; small, smooth masks she carved from scraps of peachwood and juniper; multi-colored strips of cloth she wove into quilts that told stories. Her last quilt had been the story of a splintered woman struggling to become whole.

She wore her wig easily at the market. She never felt confused in her stall with her wig on; never felt as she did most other times, when she couldn't quite figure out who anyone was, least of all herself.

▼▲▼▲▼

For a while, Reba didn't know who God was. She knew God was not the blond-haired, blue-eyed man whose picture hung larger than life behind Reverend Gary's pulpit.

It was a mystery to her: all those bronze, open faces glistening with reverence in the church. Sister Eileen twisting, shouting, and falling to the floor, writhing every Sunday, dress hiked up to her hips, showing meaty thighs, stocking tops, the lycra of her girdle—everything an eye might not want to see. And Reverend Gary ignoring her and the others as he preached faster and faster about the holy spirit, until the whole congregation was in a holy uproar, jumping, fanning, and sweating before collapsing on the pews, wet and spent.

But Reba knew it wasn't the holy spirit who had slipped its hand from her waist to her blossoming behind during fellowship. She knew it was that slick-hipped Reverend Gary. No, Reba knew God was not to be found in that church.

Her Aunt Nita, though, had acted as if Reba had blasphemed when her niece stopped going to her church. The Gospel was all Nita Garrett had ever known and she was satisfied with that, so when some folks came together and decided to build their own colored church, they built it right up around Nita's house because she was already Pearl's secret temple. She'd sit up in the front pew of the church on any night and have a talk with God about people's problems. No one knew exactly what she said because she always sounded as if she were mumbling.

But Reba had always known her Aunt Nita was talking her spirit talk.

Everyone knew that when anyone got sick, all they

needed to do was go to Nita Garrett's and ask her to have a special talk with her Lord. Jennie Mae Wilcox had gone to see Nita. Jennie Mae Wilcox had thought her husband had left her and their five children and headed north. It turned out that Nate was in his pickup headed for Chicago when he heard a whisper in his ear just outside Memphis, telling him to go back home. And he did.

Then Reba thought she found God in the stones she found near the river and in the whistling of the streams. She wanted to have that inner shining of Aunt Nita's to guide her through the stark days when there was no one to talk to and everyone asked her, "What are you?"

She'd slip down to the river without Viola ever knowing. It was there, with the moon's eyes watching and the leaves rustling and the rippling of the water that she first started painting her nude body with the muddy red clay.

At first she was shy, streaking only her fingers, arms, and long legs with russet. As she gradually felt more at home on the riverbank, she became bolder, covering her entire body with mud.

She was especially careful around her pubis, as she wanted it sacredly adorned. She weaved small twigs through her hairs and smeared them with silky veneer. She felt dark and powerful then. She never wore her wig at the river.

She'd massage the clay into her bald scalp until her lacquered head was a mirror of the bright red moon, then she'd lay on her bed of thick, dank moss and open her legs to the night.

▼▲▼▲▼

Late one night, she stayed in her stall long after the other merchants had stored their goods and gone home.

As she sat on her stool gently calling forth an old brown face from the slickened juniper she held carefully in her hands, lulling the image from the wood with the gentle pull of her fingers and the sharp-edged cutting blade, a short, wide-chested, ivory-colored man stepped from the shadows into the light of her green eyes.

"What you got there?"

"You got to come back in the morning. We closed up now."

"Your eyes open. And your lips."

Reba looked hard at the man: the halo of dark hair, the ages lined in his broad features, the night-filled eyes. But it was the crinkly wild growth of hair, like sweetgrass, that covered his chin and cheeks; in fact, the entire lower half of his face was covered with black hair. It was the wildness of that hair that kept Reba's lips from directing some sharp-tipped words into those nighteyes.

"You got to come back. We closed now."

"I got to...?" the man teased.

"If you want to know what I got."

"I know what you got, but are you gonna give it to me?" The man laughed as he stepped back and melted into the night.

He returned the next evening just about closing time. Reba was folding her quilts and putting them into the storage bin when he walked into her stall.

"How much is this one?" he asked pointing to a multi-colored cotton quilt that told the story of a lost boy with no skin and how he eventually disappeared into the red appliqué at the lower righthand corner.

"What's it worth to you?"

"My life, but I ain't gonna pay that price."

"You crazy?"

"Ain't you?" he asked with his dark eyes grinning.

And they laughed: his a deep rolling chuckle, and Reba's long rusty gulps, her laughter, a surprise.

"That quilt's reasonable."

"But are you?" he asked, still smiling. "I can't stand no reasonable woman."

Reba looked hard at him again. His wide body stood like a question between them and she didn't know how to fix her lips to answer.

Reba knew his name in her heart and sang it like an old holy song, "Rafael, Rafael, Rafael..."

She didn't know how important his evening visits to her stall were until he didn't come by one night, or the next, or the next...

Reba finally stopped looking for him to ever come back. She missed the crazy way he'd had of making her questions seem like answers, and his answers, questions. She missed the softness that was him, and the light touch of his hands on her quilts and masks, the way he held them as if he had made them himself.

Reba had started dreaming then—about Viola and Rafael, and her daddy. Long, stretched-out dreams about hands and singing voices and windows with bars.

"Tell me one of the dreams," he had asked. "Just like it feels when you're dreaming it."

Reba had closed her eyes and sat for a few minutes without moving or making a sound. And then she began.

"I am dreaming with my eyes open. I see a nurse reaching inside a blanket that moves against my skin like a wire bouquet. I rub until my skin falls like scattering leaves but she is coming for me, reaching. I fall back into the starched sheets, deep inside this dream, then rise like my flowering skin and fall onto the floor. The nurse squats beside me, grunting as she lifts. In the olive-coated walls of this dream I am my father, birthing. The nurse opens her eyes and is birthing beside me, my grunts manly, sweeter and softer than hers. The nurse holds a cup half-empty with promise. In her palms lie two sacred stones. She is smiling. My eyes are open and I am dreaming. A mountain as old as the sea rises behind me, rumbling. I close my eyes and see my mother. She is older than I have ever imagined. She shapes her lips into a song. She is singing a language only the nurse will know. I open my eyes and see the white square, cool and crisp as the bedsheets. The fingers of my mother's hands curve into a temple, an envelope lies inside, a soft and simple prayer. I open my eyes and I am dreaming. The stones fall into my mouth. My tongue rises like a rolling sea and I am choking, the taste of a thousand walls inside my mouth. I close my eyes and see my mother. She rises in my third eye like the ancient Tree of Life. She reaches for me with her armlike branches and pulls me inside where all is green. My eyes are open and I am dreaming. I move toward the horizon, a ribbon shimmering beyond these walls. I open my eyes and touch a deep, primal chord within. I am dreaming and the nurse is a liquid cord of light, opening as she encircles me-inside-my-father. I take a step and we are all dancing, the tree and the naked light inside me."

"The quilt."

Reba had looked at Rafael as if he had lost his mind.

"What quilt?"

"Look at your quilt bout that splintered woman. Looks like she finally getting herself whole."

▼▲▼▲▼

A month had passed, and one evening Reba was sitting at her stall rubbing fabric between her fingers and humming with her eyes closed when she felt him ease up in front of her.

Reba kept her eyes closed. She sensed him touching one of her new quilts.

"A bald-headed singing woman. Now how's this story gonna end?"

"Don't know yet. Don't plan no endings. Just see what happens under my fingers."

"Wonder what lovin a woman with no hair is like?"

Reba opened her eyes and looked at Rafael. With her eyes she touched his thick lips, wide ivory nose, and bushy eyebrows before answering his question by taking off her wig.

Reba closed her stall and they walked carefully that night to the river.

When they came upon her moss bed, they stripped lazily and coated their bodies with clay. When Reba finally pressed her face into the wild hair on Rafael's face, a surge of light flared inside her.

She stroked between his legs with her tongue, tasting the woods and earth there. He gently twisted the tiniest twigs he could find into Reba's pubic hairs and then stood her in the light of the moon.

He licked her toes, the balls of her feet and her ankles, before easing his tongue to her calves and knees. His fingers sought the moistness joining her thighs.

Reba moaned like the night wind in the trees. Rafael pulled her to his chest and they sank into each other, twisting in the dewy mud, pale legs wrapped around the other, shimmering on mossy sheets.

The old river watched this ritual, the crowning of desire, the flash of eyes, saying, "Yes, yes. I know what you are."

NEGRIL

ess than a quarter tank, Negril thought as he looked at the gas gauge and felt his stomach tighten. He braced himself to meet his mother inside the lopsided, rickety apartment building where she lived.

For as long as he could remember, his mother had stood before him cold as the wall of sandstone blocks where his Dogon forefathers lived. She always looked at him in her piercing way and called him the Devil, while pulling a gray shawl around her fading, loosening shoulders.

After parking his car on the street in front of his mother's building, he eased the narrow beams of his frame inside the tired wooden entryway, careful not to kick the steps with the keen toes of his day-old Florsheim's shoes as he ran up the steps to the second floor.

There was no sign of his mother when he let himself inside her apartment, and the waiting silence welcomed him as he walked toward the sagging couch. The only other piece of furniture in the tiny room was the small handcarved table standing near the far wall that held a crystal bowl filled with pink water, a fat white candle, four small polished stones, and a miniature yellow glass hen. His mother's statue of Our Lady of Candelaria sat on a square of white cloth.

"Why don't you get rid of that stuff?" he'd often asked

his mother. "It gives me the creeps," he'd say, turning away from the statue and stones and his mother kneeling before them, muttering.

"What protection do I have against Death and the Devil?" his mother would always say before turning her back and returning to her fevered whisperings.

Now, Negril turned his back to Our Lady as he threw himself onto the sofa to wait for his mother.

"Are you still going to take me to the rummage sale?" Negril's mother asked as she shook him awake.

Negril slowly focused his eyes and saw his mother peering down at him. He nodded and slowly stood. Neither of them spoke as they left the apartment and walked to the street.

"The chariot of the Devil," his mother muttered as she climbed into Negril's car.

"Oh, I don't know, Ma. I kind of imagine the Devil driving something a lot slicker than this. You know, something big and black and shiny, with lots of red leather and chrome," Negril said and then laughed.

His mother looked at him, but said nothing.

The big church rummage sale was an important event for his mother.

Negril drifted from his mother's side as soon as he saw her nod and smile at one of her friends. It was only his mother and her friends and neighbors who insisted he had the Evil Eye. The women he knew treated him as if his turquoise eyes were enchanted wish-granting stones. But the women at the church were as stern as his mother, as unsmiling as the huge wooden statue of Jesus.

"Maybe I should stick nails through my wrists and hammer myself onto her bedroom door," Negril thought to himself.

It was then the woman caught his eye.

Negril had never seen this woman before. Her skin looked as if it had been torn from the bark of some ancient tree and carved into the face looking at him. She looked older than old to Negril, and yet her eyes—there was something about her eyes. Her eyes weren't filmy like his mother's or her friends'. Looking into her eyes was like looking into a well with no bottom, or a sky with no stars, no moon. Her eyes were eternal, ancient worlds circling without end.

She looked at Negril and nodded her head. Negril jerked his eyes from the strange woman and looked around uneasily for his mother. The woman approached him.

"She has never saved you before. Why do you look for her now?" she asked and then gave a high, piercing roar that went through his ears like a dart.

"You are not afraid of an old woman like me?" she asked and laughed again.

Negril's head vibrated as if it were filled with the buzzing of a swarm of bees.

"Listen carefully now. The way has been set. Now you must place your foot upon the path."

Negril looked at the woman and thought she must be senile.

"I don't know what you're talking about."

"You think your mother does not like you. But she does not understand you, your difference. She looks at you and sees only a black and blue wound. You are more than a scar. I can see what you are, clearly, in your eyes. Your eyes are my eyes. I see the song inside you," she said. Negril turned and walked away.

When he was on the other side of the church, far away from that woman, he still did not see his mother, but he did spot a bag the woman had left in a corner by the steps leading out of the church.

Negril looked around quickly to make sure no one was looking in his direction, then he walked over to the bag, grabbed it, and ran out of the church.

Negril set the brown shopping bag on the passenger seat. He looked inside. There was a bundle of balled newspaper inside the bag and there, at the bottom, lay a mask.

The mask had the face of a man and the face of an animal, a bull with short horns at its temples. Growing from the top of the mask was a red horn that curved to the right and a black horn that curved to the left. Half of the face was red, the other half, black. The wide, open nose was tri-colored: black, white, and red. The mouth opened into a huge scream. The eyes were amber slits. The mask was made of ebony and glowed from the dark lustre of the grain. It felt hot when Negril picked it up and held it in his hands.

"When is my luck ever going to change?" he asked the mask.

The mask's eyes glowed amber. Negril put the mask to his face. He pushed his nose into the smooth wood, pressed his lips against the O of the screaming mouth.

Negril took off the mask and gunned his engine as his mother removed the shopping bag from the seat and sat beside him. She twisted her lips as if she wanted to spit. Negril jerked the car out of the parking lot and into the street. His mother filled the car with the sound of her low-voiced mutters as they sped toward her home.

Negril glanced at the quickly passing wood-framed houses leaning into each other, the spindly, recently planted saplings lining the road, the turquoise cape of sky that

mirrored the brilliance of his own eyes, and felt an inex-
plicable longing. For a moment he did not hear the
muttering of his mother. He heard the slap of skin on
water. The fluttering of arms as they struggled not to go
down. The trust in the shout of his name, "Negrilll,
Negrilll."

He looked quickly at his mother. When had his eyes
become a sign of evil to her? He did not want to remember.
He pushed the memory of that slap, the flutter of those
arms, his young brother's trust in his name, pushed that
memory into a blue-black spot inside his belly and a sound
forced its way out of that dark place, up into his lungs,
through his constricted throat, and poured over his lips,
oo-bah-dah oo-bah-dah-oh, oo-bah-dah oo-bah-dah-oh.

Negril's mother stopped muttering and visibly tightened
her body.

"Stop it. I don't ever want to hear that sound again,"
she said and resumed her muttering.

Negril closed his mouth.

Just as he turned the car into the lot behind his mother's
tired apartment building, a crow flew against the window
on Negril's side of the car. He flinched from the impact
of the bird against the glass and slammed his foot on the
brakes. His mother screamed and made the sign of the
cross.

"You know what this means, don't you? You know what
this means?" his mother cawed like the crows standing
on wires above their heads.

"Yeah, I know what it means. It means that I'm going
to have to drive around with cardboard in my window,
that's what it means."

"No," his mother cawed. "The bird, another dead bird.
First that small one that flew into the front room win-

dow last week and now this one. Death is coming," his mother cried as she scurried into the building.

"Better him dead than me," Negril said as he drove away from his mother's home.

His encounter with his mother and the old woman had left an ache inside Negril that penetrated his being as intensely as the fatigue he felt from his job of hammering slabs of Sheetrock onto walls.

Instead of showering, Negril decided to take a bath, to try to soak away the heaviness threatening to engulf him. But as he sat in the tub with pearls of sweat dribbling from his scalp, the sound again poured from his mouth, *oo-bah-dah oo-bah-dah-oh.*

As Negril sang to himself, he rocked in the water, and as he rocked and soaped his muscled black calves and thighs, his floating penis, his furry chest and long arms, he sang the words louder into the steam and his own hungry ears, *oo-bah-dah oo-bah-dah-oh,* until he did not know if the water on his face was steam or sweat or his own salty tears.

He allowed himself to remember. The softness of his young mother's smile, the warmth of her embrace. The limp brown body of his younger brother in his mother's arms. The frenzied mouths of the circling women chattering like signifying monkeys, reproach in every glare directed at him, the one black boy with the eerie-colored eyes. The endless blame heaped on his shoulders, heavy as the world.

He remembered his mother's moans, the women telling her that this damage had been brought by the evil in Negril's eyes, eyes that could move over a body like fingers. Cool, blue fingers.

He saw his brother fall again slowly, slowly, into the

opening arms of the lake. Felt the chill of the empty air in his outstretched arms, his screaming mouth.

"I had you for him," his mother had cried. "I had you to protect him, always."

"No," a hushed voice said in his ear, holding him gently against the chill then coating his world. He had looked into blue eyes in a black face like his own. "You were born for more than that. Much more. One day you will use the pain you hold inside to heal. In healing others, you will heal yourself."

It tired Negril to remember his brother's drowning and the way his mother used to love him. When he stood in the bathtub, his left foot slipped on the porcelain bottom and the tub reached up to grab his behind as he fell. His head hit the back rim of the tub.

"Son of a ...!"

"Not in my house! Not in my house!" The voice of his mother screamed inside his mind as he gingerly eased himself out of the tub.

Negril wrapped a coarse towel around his body and went to lie on the sofa. He reached for the shopping bag and pulled out the mask.

"What a gift," he groaned and stretched out on his sofa with the mask on top of his face.

▼▲▼▲▼

He opens his eyes. On the ceiling above him is a mirror. In the mirror is the face and body of a man who is also an animal, a four-legged animal with two faces—one man, one animal with four horns coming out of its head. The animal body and the man body are one. Matted black fur covers the stomach of the man/beast. A short tail curls from its coccyx. Negril looks into the eyes of the animal/man in the ceiling mirror and screams. He is looking into his own eyes. Negril screams again when the man/animal that is him falls from the mirror into his body and then they all fall deep into the center of a mountain, which is the center of the earth. After dropping past old tree roots, through the mouth of an ancient river, then falling deep below the sea, Negril hits bottom. He hears the snarling of a pack of wolves who quickly tear into his animal/man body with sharp yellow teeth, tearing each limb from his body. He watches his right arm leave his body, his left leg, a thigh. He tries to scream again, but no sound leaves what remains of his body. The wolves do not stop until every piece of him lies in a circle. Negril loses his eyes at the precise moment the leader of the wolfpack lunges for his throat. And yet, he does not die. He soon hears the cackle of the old woman, the same hushed voice he heard in his ear when his brother drowned in the lake. As he lies there in pieces, the sound of bees buzzing fills his ears, the old woman laughing. "Now are you ready?" she asks and laughs and laughs. She walks toward the head that is Negril and the man/animal. "Here, eat this. It will give you the courage you have never had, it will turn you into a man." She holds a bowl of something steaming in her gnarled hands, hands as withered and broken as the roots of a tree. She holds the bowl to his lips in those hands. Her skin is jet black, the exact shade of the wood of the mask Negril brought home from his mother's church. Around her neck is a necklace. A necklace of yellowed human teeth. That is all she wears. Those glowing teeth on her jet black skin. She holds the bowl steaming in her rootlike hands. Negril looks inside the bowl but cannot scream. The old woman makes her hands into a spoon and puts a large handful of the steaming mess into Negril's mouth. Negril tells himself over and over no, this

is not human waste. When she is satisfied he has eaten enough,
she gathers his limbs around his head and pieces him back
together. At the end, when he is almost whole, she sticks her
hand into the breast of the lead wolf. Gently, she places the
heart of the wolf into the empty space of Negril. "Here, this
is what you've been missing. Remember now, you are a man,
a man with the power to heal. I watch you always. And I
will come again if you step from the path that has been set."
The ancient woman laughs until the teeth around her neck
rattle and Negril's ears once again fill with the roar of
thousands upon thousands of bees.

▼▲▼▲▼

Negril opened his eyes slowly. His body was flooded
with sweat. He stretched a leg, flexed a toe. He wiggled
his arms and shook his fingers. He held his neck in his
hands. Everything was as it should be. For the first time
in his tired life, a glimmer of hope snaked through his
black body. He hugged himself. Then, smiling, he reached
for the mask, but it was gone.

EMERALD CITY: THIRD & PIKE

This is Oya's corner. The pin-striped young executives and sleek-pumped clerk-typists, the lacquered-hair punk boys and bleached blondes with safety pins dangling from multi-holed earlobes, the frantic-eyed woman on the corner shouting obscenities, and the old-timers rambling past new high-rise fantasy hotels—all belong to Oya even though she's the only one who knows it.

Oya sits on this corner 365 days of the year, in front of the new McDonald's, with everything she needs bundled inside two plastic bags by her side. Most people pretend they don't even see Oya sitting there like a Buddha under that old green Salvation Army blanket.

Sometimes Oya's eyes look red and wild, but she won't say anything to anybody. Other times her eyes are flat, black and still as midnight outside the mission, and she talks up a furious wind.

She tells them about her family—her uncle who was a cowboy, her grandfather who fought in the Civil War, her mother who sang dirges and blues songs on the Chitlin Circuit, and her daddy who wouldn't "take no stuff from nobody," which is why they say some people got together and broke his back.

"Oh yeah, Oya be tellin them folks an earful if they'd ever stop to listen, but she don't pay em no mind. Just keeps right on talkin, keeps right on tellin it."

One day when Oya's eyes were flat and black and she was in a preaching mood, I walked down Third & Pike, passed her as if I didn't know her. Actually I didn't. But Oya turned her eyes on me and I could feel her looking at me and I knew I couldn't just walk past this woman without saying something. So I said, "Hello."

Oya looked at me with those flat black eyes and motioned for me to take a seat by her.

Now, usually I'm afraid of folks who sit on the sidewalks downtown and look as if they've never held a job or have no place to go, but something about her eyes made me sit.

I felt foolish. I felt my face growing warm and wondered what people walking by must think of me sitting on the street next to this woman who looked as if she had nowhere to go. But after sitting there for a few minutes, it seemed as if they didn't think more or less of me than when I was walking down the street. No one paid any attention to us. That bothered me. What if I really needed help or something? What if I couldn't talk, could only sit on that street?

"Don't pay them fools no mind, daughter. They wouldn't know Moses if he walked down Pike Street and split the Nordstrom Building right down the middle. You from round here?"

I nodded my head.

"I thought so. You look like one of them folks what's been up here all they lives, kinda soft-lookin like you ain't never knowed no hard work."

I immediately took offense because I could feel the

inevitable speech coming on: "There ain't no real black people in Seattle."

"Calm down, daughter, I don't mean to hurt your feelings. It's just a fact, that's all. You folks up here too cushy, too soft. Can't help it. It's the rainwater does it to you, all that water can't help but make a body soggy and spineless."

I made a move to get up.

"Now wait a minute, just wait a minute. Let me show you somethin."

She reached in her pocket and pulled out a crumpled newspaper clipping. It held a picture of a grim-faced young woman and a caption that read: "DOMESTIC TO SERVE TIME IN PRISON FOR NEAR-MURDER."

"That's me in that picture. Now ain't that somethin?"

Sure is, I thought and wondered how in the world I would get away from this woman before she hurt me.

"Them fools put me in the jail for protectin my dreams. Humph, they the only dreams I got, so naturally I'm gonna protect em. Nobody else gonna do it for me, is they?"

"But how could somebody put you in jail for protectin your dreams? That paper said you almost killed somebody."

I didn't want to seem combative but I didn't know exactly what this lady was talking about and I was feeling pretty uneasy after she'd almost insulted me then showed me evidence she'd been in jail for near-murder, no less.

"Now, I know you folks up here don't know much bout the importance of a body's dreams, but where I come from dreams was all we had. Seemed like a body got holt of a dream or a dream got holt of a body and wouldn't turn you loose. My dreams what got me through so many days of nothin, specially when it seemed like the only thing the future had to give was more of the same nothin, day after day."

She stopped abruptly and stared into space. I kept wondering what kind of dream would have forced her to try to kill somebody.

"Ain't nothin wrong with cleanin other folks' homes to make a livin. Nothin wrong with it at all. My mama had to do it and her mama had to do it at one time or nuther, so it didn't bother me none when it turned out I was gonna hafta do it too, least for a while. But my dream told me I wasn't gonna wash and scrub and shine behind other folks the rest of my life. Jobs like that was just temporary, you know what I mean?"

I nodded my head.

"Look at my hands. You never woulda knowed I danced in one of them fancy colored nightclubs and wore silk evenin gloves. Was in a sorority. Went to Xavier University."

As she reminisced, I looked at her hands. They looked rough and wide, like hands that had seen hard labor. I wondered if prison had caused them to look that way.

Oya's eyes pierced into mine. She seemed to know what I was thinking. She cackled.

"Daughter, they'd hafta put more than a prison on me to break my spirit. Don't you know it takes more than bars and beefy guards to break a fightin woman's spirit?"

She cackled some more.

"Un Un. Wouldn't never break me, and they damn sure tried. I spent fifteen years in that hellhole. Fifteen years of my precious life, all for a dreamkiller."

I looked at her and asked, "But what did you do? What did they try to do to your dreams?"

93

Oya leaned over to me and whispered, "I was gonna get into the space program. I was gonna be a astronaut and fly out into the universe, past all them stars. I was gonna meet up with some folks none of us never seen before, and be ambassador of goodwill; not like the fools bein sent out there now thinkin they own the universe. I was gonna be a real ambassador of goodwill and then that woman I scrubbed floors for had the nerve to tell me no black maid was ever gonna be no astronaut. Well, I could feel all the broken dreams of my mama and my grand-mama and her mama swell up and start pulsin in my blood memory. I hauled off and beat that fool over the head with the mop I had in my hands till I couldn't raise up my arms no more. The chantin of my people's broken dreams died down and I looked and there was that dreamkiller in a mess of blood all over the clean floor I'd just scrubbed. And they turned round and put me in jail and never did say nothin bout that old dreamkiller. Just like my dreams never mattered. Like I didn't have no dreams. Like all I could ever think bout doin was cleanin up after nasty white folks for the rest of my life.

"Humph!" She snorted, and I almost eased to my feet so I could run if I had the cause to.

"You got any dreams, daughter?" Oya asked with a gleam in her eye.

I knew I better tell her yes, so I did.

"Well I don't care if you is from up here, you better fight for your dreams!"

Slowly, I reached out and held one of her rough hands. Then I asked, "But was your dream worth going to prison for all them years?"

Oya looked at me for a long, long time.

"I'm still gonna make it past all them stars," she said

as she freed her hand and motioned for me to get to getting.

"Right now, this street b'longs to me and don't *nobody* mess with me or my dreams!" She was still shouting as I walked toward Pine Street.

Talking Mountain

agdalena has no tongue. She walks through the streets of this town with her mouth on fire. She is burning inside, the liquid glow of her skin afire, a soul trying to rise to the surface. A small group of children follow slowly behind her, grunting, aping the sounds Magdalena makes with her piglike, closed-up mouth. She does not see the children, does not look behind her skirts flowing like a soft black river. She wears no shoes on her tough, wide feet, feet that move over glass and stone as if they were cushions of down.

It was a pair of hands that took her tongue, a soft wide pair of hands. Hands that held a sharp yellow pencil firmly between tense slender fingers, hands that could turn soft while holding a brush for painting; a brush to be dipped into small round pots of color, paint to be slapped across a canvas wild with life. Magdalena could be such a canvas, her body a long blank cloth to be splashed with design.

Her story is old, and Magdalena's soul was ancient when Tavio first sat in her classroom, all of his sixteen years bunched up inside his tall frame like a tight black fist. Before he had sat in the stiff-backed wooden chair in her room, Magdalena had looked into the dull eyes of countless numbers of children, eyes that were small worlds that passed like her days, eternal barren planets on parade. Unlike the others, Tavio listened carefully to her every lesson. Her every pronouncement rang inside his ears like bellringing edicts from God. His eyes seeped below the surface of her skin, searching. Searching for the woman that was Magdalena, the woman inside the rustles of long, black, draped skirts she wore as if swathed in mourning.

"Open your eyes to me, woman," Tavio's eyes seemed to tell her.

Magdalena became distracted during her lessons. This was something she had never expected: to be looked at as if she were a woman on fire, listened to as if her every thought were a precious, shimmering jewel.

She could not look directly into the eyes of this boy-man; her eyes would flit around the room like small, dark birds in a cage, a cage whose walls were shrinking; but she, Magdalena, was growing larger, much too large for the walls of this classroom, the tired coupling with the principal, the dark eyes of the boy burning inside her, the cage of her heavy dark dress.

Soon, she loomed within her mind's eye, larger than life, larger than the statue of the Virgin standing at the foot of Talking Mountain, larger even than Jesus.

Magdalena was no virgin. She knew what to do with a man's body, with a man's hands stroking her tight, dark skin.

"But Tavio is not yet a man," a small voice whined inside her head. She pushed the drone of that voice down inside her, deep where she would not be disturbed.

Then, one day when Magdalena had grown as large as she could possibly grow in this cottonbowl of a city, this gray-dappled, wide-flanked, one-horse town, she took Tavio inside her dark skirts, inside the cage that was her body; she took him there where the small sweet Magdalena rested, deep inside where the mountains talked and spit fire, where a river flowed with hot dark foam, underground. Magdalena took Tavio to a place no one had ever been before inside her, not even her sad-eyed husband, a place where each particle of her flesh was a wild singing song.

The sound of Tavio's and Magdalena's deep, primal song drowned out the creaking of the heavy wooden classroom door as it opened, opened to another world where eyes as old and dark as Magdalena's looked upon the two naked bodies twisting and singing, their flesh glowing with dew from each other.

And then, at the precise moment that the lava of Tavio joined with Magdalena's own boiling flames, at the precise point where she was all desire, and free, the mouth on the face belonging to the eyes from the other world opened there in the doorway of Magdalena's classroom, that mouth opened and made the sound of a mountain choking, a tall smoking mountain choking, like a man who cannot spit.

Tavio had seen this choking, sputtering man many times before, speaking with authority, moving easily through the rooms of this school as if they were his own small, dark kingdom.

Tavio looked into the eyes of this man and saw something breaking inside them, earth crumbling and falling in upon itself, trees coming up out of the ground by the roots. And Tavio was afraid.

The man reached for Tavio with arms as long and sharp as broken branches, but he, the boy not yet a man, ran buttocks aglow from the room as quickly and surely as his hard dark sixteen years. Leaving the song that was Magdalena in the hands of the man with the breaking eyes, who put those hands, hands the priest had blessed, his married-sad-tired hands, now circling the neck of Magdalena, pressing inside her mouth, hands reaching for her love tongue as she struggled against the cage of her body, against the wide hands breaking the cage, against the shrinking walls of the room, her shriveling body, a body that is old now, older even than Talking Mountain.

A Season

I

She is circling, Chango, ever circling. I feel Her in the wind, hanging low over trees, silvery with light. She moans like a woman lost, Chango, deep and full of pleasure even when the hills scream and the days move as slowly as Benito's burro who is almost bald now and blind from the heat. Her belly twitches from a spasm of love. But we must not speak of that now, Chango. Now, there are only days stretching before us. No end to the horizon and this silence. Chango, always this silence.

You would never have known I was a girl who loved to run, Chango, loved to feel the wind between my legs, soaring, the brown dirt turning, my bare feet like wheels and I would move so fast my people thought I might disappear, just vanish into the trees and the silence like a brown wind, me, running, flying, melting into the line at the edge of the earth and sea, running in the Island of Pines, Chango, before I came here.

Sometimes I think we are such poor people since all we have are our stories, and other times, Chango, I think how very rich we are.

The sun stretched its summery fingers into autumn and caressed the lean backs of the workers. The fruit, full of promise, gleamed in the sun. A woman walked past the fields, past the workers who perpetually stretched their arms. The muscles in their bodies held the stories.

Did I ever tell you how much my mother loved to cry? Over anything, Chango, any sign of life, any twinkling or glimmering of sorrow or joy and her tears would fall. A mass for the dead, first communion, and slowly, surely, her eyes would fill with water, tears sliding down her cheeks like pearls of salt.

She was a big woman, Chango, much bigger than me. They thought my father a rich man because his wife was so big and everyone else was small, small like me.

But when she cried, my mother's breasts shook like a fat man's laughing belly. And her mouth opened wide, her lips were full and the color of pomegranates, Chango, pomegranates loaded on the farmer's oxcarts. Her teeth were very white, and strong just like the rest of her.

The sound of her crying would flood the valley and roll out to the sea. It would flow from inside her, from somewhere deep in her stomach the sound would come out like all of the sounds of the world balled fistlike into her crying.

Ah oo um ah oo um is kind of how it sounded, Chango, like if you close your eyes and listen to the sound of the universe breathing, that was the sound of my mother's tears.

She is circling Chango, always circling. I can feel her flying low to the ground, her belt of skulls rattling in the wind. The sound of wind whistling through the cracks of our house is Her, Chango. She moves through the air like blood flowing in our veins, Chango. She moves in us like blood.

II

The sun pressed the workers into the hardening earth. The workers continued their eternal dance in and out of the fields. Sweat covered the brown fruit of their bodies. A worker left the field of bent men, the never ending yawn of the earth. The story inside his body pushed him along the road.

They would tell us in the camps only a woman would run, Maya, only a woman. I still do not understand why it took me so long. I was seven when they snatched me. I cannot tell you the sound of my father's laughter. My mother died pushing me from her womb, Maya. She died to give me life. I have felt her eyes watching, seeing what I had become.

I could only pick half a bushel, Maya. Half a bushel for my milk and bread. I was dead at seven, Maya, but still walking and breathing and taking life, moving from camp to camp. I have never been so dead as when I killed, Maya.

There are things in me that can only be said in dreams.

When I was young and alive, I remember putting my head to the ground near the mountain at the edge of the fields and hearing a whisper rise from the core of the earth, Maya, a whisper rising. I could hear the sound darkness makes. There, deep in the earth: *ah oo um ah oo um ah oo um,* a deep swirling hum. I promised myself when I became a man I would follow that sound wherever it might lead me.

Death is not an ugly thing, Maya, it is the killing that will take your soul.

They took me to their camps when I was seven. There were other boys my age from different places. The first thing they had us do, Maya, was kill a lamb. Five of us had to chase the lamb and catch it, pulling it down to the ground where we used our hands to take its breath. Their guns looked like cannons pointed at our temples.

I got the heart, Maya. I knew the very instant his breath stopped. I will never get the sound of his rattle from my ears. Even now in dreams I see his eyes shining.

And when I had to kill men, Maya, I thought of them as lambs, always taking the heart.

The man and woman walked the road into a changing season, stories fresh on their lips, like fruit. Tonight, the Harvest Moon will cover the timeless dance of their bodies with an umber glow.

III

I had never seen a man with so much stillness inside, Chango. So much quiet is in your eyes.

I am a cavefish, Maya. I move, love, feed in the dark. With you, my bones soften and I can just be skin. The darkness of your skin warms me, Maya. There is a light within your skin, glowing, a flame between your skin and bones that makes me warm.

The days you are gone I pretend that you never were, Chango, that our eyes never caught and held like paper between flint and steel. Do you remember the first glance in the fields? Even then She was circling.

Have you tasted your own blood, Maya, or seen fresh blood pouring from an open wound?

I have heard the screams, Chango. I have seen the blood of my mother drying in the sun, the same blood that turned my father into stone. That is the blood I have seen, Chango, that, and the screams are enough.

IV

Take my hand.
What?
Take my hand, woman, we are going to dance.
You are wild with heat, Chango.

Put your ear to the ground. Do you hear it? The sound of water and darkness?

It must be too far down.

No.

Too deep.

No. Listen with your heart. Open your ears to the sound, Maya.

Do YOU hear it?

It is what keeps me alive. Give me your hand. Listen.

Ah oo um ah oo um ah oo um ah oo um, that is the sound, Maya, the sound of the earth humming, the sound of peace, of your mother's tears. Now move.

What?

Let your hips sway to the sound, feel it flowing in your veins *ah oo um ah oo um ah oo um.* Pick up your feet and put them back down heavy like a man coming in from the fields, or a woman walking miles with a water jug on her head, move them like you are digging yourself back into the earth, back into your mother, back home where silence is paradise and there are no fields no guns no children growing into machines. Move your hips like there is a future and there is a great joy in knowing you are a woman and I a man, *ah oo um ah oo um ah oo um ah oo um.* Now slowly start to move in a circle, feel the weight lifting from your arms, your back. Your spine is rising toward the sun. The tears falling from your eyes are your mother's tears bathing you with joy. See how she laughs in her tears? Feel the cleansing softness, how bright the light from her eyes, the warmth of her love. Now spin faster, watch the earth turn beneath your feet, a brown blur of light ascending your legs, and you are one with earth and light and your mother's tears, *ah oo um ah oo um ah oo um.* You raise your arms above your head and you are healed with the sight and sound, with the salt of earth, *ah oo um ah oo um ah oo um ah oo um ah oo um ah oo um ah oo um ah oo um.*

V

This is a time of silence, a time my tongue cannot sound the language of your eyes, black moons beckoning. It is a time when all around us is filled with no sound our hearts can speak, the rhythm of trees, of flowers folding unto themselves. This is the season with no name.

You come to this womb easily, Chango.
It is time
The sun slips from the sky easy as a red dress
from your shoulders
Is anyone near?
I am all you have to fear
This is no easy feat, this small moment in the eyes of
the gods
Your muscles curve around the bone, Chango
The cleavage of these brown hills will warm us
Even the stiff-winged birds soften in this heat
But not you, Chango
I am the rock in the river, unbroken
I am the water sliding through
Your nipples murmur
With you I am a river singing

And I, the rock in the middle
Are those footsteps?
All you have to fear are my lips at the base of your
spine,
circling
The easy parting of the trees
Sweet grasses beneath our feet
Your tongue in my ear
All of this roar in a world filled with silence, Chango
Your softening breasts in my hands
Fingers that have held guns
Not the way I hold your sex, softly, in these hands,
stroking
Hands that have opened bodies
Easy as I am opening you now
This is not easy, Chango
I am the rock in the river, unbroken
I am the water sliding through
I take you into my mouth sweet as grass
Here in this time of silence
When my lips know no language that cannot em-
brace your eyes
And the only sound
My tooth biting into your shoulder
The sound of a river singing

CHARLOTTE WATSON SHERMAN

Charlotte Watson Sherman, a native of Seattle, received her B.A. in Social Sciences from Seattle University. She has worked as a Sexual Abuse Counselor as well as Outreach Coordinator for Seattle Rape Relief and is currently a Mental Health Specialist in Seattle. She has been writing both poetry and prose for a number of years; her publication credits include *Obsidian, The Black Scholar, CALYX Journal, Painted Bride Quarterly,* and *Ikon.* Her stories have also been included in *When I Am An Old Woman I Shall Wear Purple* (Papier Mache Press, 1988), *Memories and Visions* (Crossing Press, 1989), and *Gathering Ground* (Seal Press, 1984). The manuscript of *Killing Color* was selected by Craig Lesley for the King County Arts Commission Fiction Award in 1989. Ms. Sherman also received the 1989 Seattle Arts Commission Individual Artists Fiction Grant for her writing. She writes and lives in Seattle with her husband and two daughters.

Selected Titles from Award-Winning CALYX Books

Black Candle, by Chitra Divakaruni. Poems about women from India, Pakistan, and Bangladesh.
ISBN 0-934971-23-4, $8.95, paper; ISBN 0-934971-24-2, $16.95, cloth.

Ginseng and Other Tales from Manila, by Marianne Villanueva. Poignant short stories set in the Philippines.
ISBN 0-934971-19-6, $8.95, paper; ISBN 0-934971-20-X, $16.95, cloth.

Idleness Is the Root of All Love, by Christa Reinig, translated by Ilze Mueller. These poems by the prize-winning German poet accompany two older lesbians through a year of love and struggle.
ISBN 0-934971-21-8, $10, paper; ISBN 0-934971-22-6, $18.95, cloth.

The Forbidden Stitch: An Asian American Women's Anthology, edited by Shirley Geok-lin Lim, et. al. The first Asian American women's anthology. **Winner of the American Book Award.**
ISBN 0-934971-04-8, $16.95, paper; ISBN 0-934971-10-2, $29.95, cloth.

Women and Aging, An Anthology by Women, edited by Jo Alexander, et. al. The only anthology that addresses ageism from a feminist perspective. A rich collection of older women's voices.
ISBN 0-934971-00-5, $15.95, paper; ISBN 0-934971-07-2, $28.95, cloth.

In China with Harpo and Karl, by Sibyl James. Essays revealing a feminist poet's experiences while teaching in Shanghai, People's Republic of China.
ISBN 0-934971-15-3, $9.95, paper; ISBN 0-934971-16-1, $17.95, cloth.

Indian Singing in 20th Century America, by Gail Tremblay. A work of hope by a Native American poet.
ISBN 0-934971-13-7, $8.95, paper; ISBN 0-934971-14-5, $16.95, cloth.

The Riverhouse Stories, by Andrea Carlisle. A classic! Unlike any other lesbian novel published. A delight!
ISBN 0-934971-01-3, $8.95, paper; ISBN 0-934971-08-0, $16.95, cloth.

Florilegia, edited by Debi Berrow, et. al. A retrospective of the finest literary and artistic work published during the first decade of *CALYX, A Journal of Art and Literature by Women.*
ISBN 0-934971-06-4, $12, paper; ISBN 0-934971-09-9, $24.95, cloth.

Forthcoming Titles – 1992

Mrs. Vargas and the Dead Naturalist, by Kathleen Alcalá. Fourteen stories set in Mexico and the Southwestern U.S., written in the tradition of magical realism.
ISBN 0-934971-25-0, $9.95, paper; ISBN 0-934971-26-9, $18.95, cloth.

The Nicaraguan Women Poets Anthology, edited by Daisy Zamora. A collection of poetry by Nicaraguan women—Miskito Indian women, early 20th century poets, and better-known poets writing since the 1960s.
ISBN 0-934971-27-7, paper; ISBN 0-934971-28-5, cloth. Prices pending.

CALYX Books is committed to producing books of literary, social, and feminist integrity.

These books are available at your local bookstore or direct from:

CALYX Books, PO Box B, Corvallis, OR 97339

(Please include payment with your order. Add $1.50 postage for first book and $.75 for each additional book.)

CALYX, Inc., is a nonprofit organization with a 501(C)(3) status. All donations are tax deductible.

Colophon

Text is set in Galliard. Titles are in Lithos Bold.
Design and composition by ImPrint Services, Corvallis.